THE MORTAL

—AND THE—
CIMMERIAN SHADE

EDIE HOBER

ILLUSTRATIONS BY MELAYNA HENDERSON

authorHOUSE®

AuthorHouse™
1663 Liberty Drive
Bloomington, IN 47403
www.authorhouse.com
Phone: 1 (800) 839-8640

Published by AuthorHouse 10/23/2018

ISBN: 978-1-5462-4162-1 (sc)
ISBN: 978-1-5462-4161-4 (e)

Library of Congress Control Number: 2018906560

Print information available on the last page.

Dedicated to my family and friends, who have encouraged me to follow my dreams. A special thanks to my cousin Janeen, who helped me in editing.

CONTENTS

PROLOGUE

The Curse

Once upon a time, long ago in the forgotten moors of England, dwelled a Cimmerian (sa-meer-e-an) Shade Prince, I, Athelstan Moren. I spent two-hundred and twelve years doing as I pleased, with no consequences, turning into *The* Casanova. There was not a maiden or a gentleman who could resist my charisma and would easily fall into my bed.

My parents never appreciated how I moved through my existence, without a care in the world. My carelessness made them conclude I should take a bride. Their decree was to arrange a marriage to the mortally weak enchantress, Maida Miller. She lived from one illness to another, forcing the hand of her parents to procure her future. I loathed standing in the same room as the creature.

The whole arrangement irritated me, due to the years of studying Cimmerian laws and customs. Our law stated, if a Cimmerian married a mortal, they must be turned after wedlock. The prospect of touching this putrid girl caused my skin to crawl. I did not want to be spending my immortality with a changed mortal. I refused to spend our extended lifespan together. I rebelled against the unwanted arrangement in silent rage.

My rebellion mattered not to my folks, nor the Millers, who considered the match ingenious. What they perceived brilliant, forced me to act as if I loved marrying the loathsome creature and caused me to hide my affairs. I became brilliant in cloaking my lovers by using the secret passageways throughout the castle.

However, my Casanova ways ended, when I met my twin soul, Isadora Munez. It had become an uncommon occurrence, in the world's ever-growing population, to find one's soulmate. I regarded the discovery as my freedom from the unsought contract.

This discovery was not embraced by my parents. They informed me the contract could only be voided, if either of us were to have a baby with someone else. The prospect of my soul's other half carrying my offspring, brought me great pleasure, in more ways than one. I worked hard to implant my seed, within the body of my beloved, and became careless at hiding the affair.

My downfall came one night when my mum, Maida, and Maida's mother, Luella Miller, caught us in a lover's embrace, in a nook, on the fourth floor of the library. Heartbroken, Maida cast a spell to end her existence. I cared not, that my bride had taken her life, which looking back now, I should have. The only thing that mattered was my betrothal to my twin soul.

The announcement of my new engagement, to my beloved, was to be made after the required three weeks of mourning. They were the longest weeks of my life, however, I spent that time planning a banquet to introduce my bride to be.

During the engagement party, while we waited for my beloved to show up, my parents noticed a change in me. For the first time, in my existence, I smiled a genuine smile. It was not a forced enjoyment, or a slight smirk of revenge, but a bona fide expression of blissfulness. My mood changed when Luella walked into the Shade Castle's ballroom.

Luella held a wild look, with grey matted hair, and wore dirty, torn clothes. Her face appeared to have aged dramatically, since the death of her daughter. She tossed a burlap bag at me and said, "For the misdeeds you have brought into my home… I curse you, Prince Athelstan Kirkley Moren, to live out your days, in this palace, with no hope of escape. Only when you find your true soulmate, will the spell lift. You have until your six hundredth birthday to locate her, or die, knowing the pain caused to my only child."

The bag rolled, leaving a trail of maroon liquid, until it rested at my feet. I stared at the brown, wet mass. When my eyes moved up to Luella, she had vanished, and the room was eerily silent. Everyone gawked at me and the sack. Bending down, I picked up the bag. As I opened it and peered into the horrifying abyss, my heart froze. I could not trust what I was seeing.

I pulled out the contents as the soiled cloth fluttered to the ground;

my twin soul's head cradled in my hands. Rage filled me as my throat constricted *needing blood*. Luella's blood!

Isadora's eyes had shown horror and her lips held a silent scream. My beloved's head slipped from my fingers as I bolted after Luella. Rage consumed me as I neared the Enchantress, who stood just beyond the gates of the royal grounds. Approaching the gateway with murderous intent, the hag mere inches from my grasp, I crumpled to the ground. I laid in the entryway, paralyzed from the pain that pulsated from my chest. It was as if someone reached into my rib cage and pulverized my heart. I was there, gasping in agony, as she smiled down at me in triumph because she knew she had won.

CHAPTER 1

The Contest

The dice rolled across the board, resting on the number six. *Yes!* "Nicki," my best friend and roommate, Bridget, shouted before tossing popcorn at me, laughing, "No fair!" As I calculated how much I'd be getting for the forty-five acres of fruit, Bridget's phone started blaring "Cool for the Summer." Before I could reprimand her, she skedaddled off to her room. Slamming her door closed caused a vibration that rattled the pentagram, nearly dropping it off the door.

An hour had gone by since Bridget raced to her bedroom and I was about to clean out the bank of my favorite board game, *The Farming Game*. Bridget was always a sore loser and considered this game stupid and preferred to play *Monopoly*. But when we played *Monopoly*, she won, and I lost. I found *Monopoly* to be dumb and similar to *The Farming Game*. We took turns each week with which game to play, but sometimes she refused to play mine. Our argument ended when I told her, *I'll never play your game again, if you won't play mine.* She would usually suck it up and play the game anyway. But this was one week she didn't want to play.

There were only two rules during our weekly game night: first to get completely wasted, second no electronics allowed. Tonight, Bridget broke both rules. She refused our signature drink of vodka, orange, and grapefruit juice mixers. We would never contemplate refusing one of our concoctions.

For a while, I had sensed Bridget was hiding an agenda from me, but I could not assess her motives. Especially tonight. She'd been acting jittery and couldn't sit still to save her life. On top of that, she kept watching her phone like it was going to sprout wings and fly off. When her phone rang, her face brightened. A part of me wondered who was on the phone, while another part feared the answer.

Bridget believed in polyamorous relationships. The only problem I had with her preference is that her men didn't know she had multiple partners. I considered it cheating. She found the relationships exhilarating, while I found them to be exhausting.

I asked her once why she had secret relationships, and she responded, "A girl has needs." Then, I made the mistake in asking, "What do you mean?"

With a sly smile, she answered, "Your virgin ears wouldn't like the details."

I perked up when I caught the sound of Bridget's bedroom door opening and her running out to the card table; phone closed and a wide smile on her heart-shaped face. This look meant only one thing, it was a guy. Eyebrow raised, I asked, "Okay, that smile is not over this game, as you are losing. So, which of the guys you're dating, called?" While I don't approve of her lifestyle choices, I've learned to accept her because I'd go mental trying to change her.

Bridget's rosy, pink, silicone lips widened further, showing off her white teeth. "Neither!" She started bouncing in her spot, squealing, "It was the sponsors of a short story writing contest I entered a month ago. And you will never believe this!"

"Well, considering I didn't even know you wrote, it might be two things I don't believe." I joked, standing to pack up the game, having the sensation it was now forgotten by her.

Bridget frowned before smiling once more. "I can't write. So, I entered one of your short stories. The one you are always working on! And it won!"

I felt my face warm up and shouted, "I cannot believe you! You stole one of my stories?! Which one?!" I couldn't remember one being tampered with or missing. Either way, I felt violated and livid that she had done this. Her actions shouldn't have surprised me, since she was always butting into my life, but this went beyond asking a guy out for me. She had done this before and ended up dating the guy herself. This was more personal. It was amazing my story won the contest, but she had stolen the script and claimed it as her own. Morally, she cheated in the contest and should not have been this excited about winning. She's a thief! I couldn't state that enough times.

"Nicki, that isn't the point. The point is, your story won. You write great stories. Plus, the grand prize winner gets to go to England, and stay in an authentic castle, with a Duke! Who knows?! You might even fall in love with him," she said, getting squirmy and excited by the thought. Bridget can be exasperating. She's a hopeless romantic and had it in her head I was due for a hot steamy relationship. I begged to differ after my last long-term relationship ended. For someone who prefers multiple significant others, you'd think she'd understand my reservations. I hated using the words *significant other* to describe her relationships with men. However, spouses or boyfriends just didn't sound right.

Irritated, I shouted, "Wrong! You won the contest, not me! You are going to England, not me! And you stole my story!"

"Umm, wait! Did I not mention I get to bring a guest?"

I love my best friend. Honestly, I do. But she can be a challenge.

I blinked a few times, trying to lower my anger, "No! You didn't tell me that! Even still you stole from me. And what's worse, is that you used it in a contest." Towards the end, I whined, but I didn't care at this point because I was fuming. My eyes teared up, and I tried to keep them at bay. I failed miserably. I hated getting so mad that I would cry. I was convinced getting so upset and crying was a woman thing.

"Oh, Nicki! Who cares if I stole the story. You are finally going to England and you don't even have to pay for the flight, nor the stay, nor the food, because it's covered. Plus, you get to meet a Duke. Let's hope he is a cute Duke because the goddess only knows you need TLC," she said, with a twinkle in her eye. The twinkle that says *you're not getting out of this. So, just accept it.* I detested that twinkle.

Exasperated, I sighed, "Alright, I assume I am your number one choice for this all-expense-paid-trip to England?" I paused for a reply, only to have her smile and nod. "Great, when do we leave?"

I don't think I have ever seen Bridget so excited about something. She squealed, "Tomorrow at noon!"

"Ok, fine. We need to gather things for... wait a minute. Are you kidding me? That's not enough time to get ready! We need passports, wash clothes, let our jobs know we will be out of town, and...," I started to hyperventilate as my anxiety levels began to rise.

Bridget, sensing my rising panic, interrupted, "Chill-lax, will ya? It's all taken care of. I got passports ages ago, when I entered the contest, because I figured with your story there was no way we'd lose. While I was talking with the sponsor of the contest about the things we'd need to buy in order to be ready by tomorrow at noon, he said we need to bring shower junk and other feminine products because they are supplying us with everything else. I am talking shoes, undergarments and get this... a wardrobe!" She tried a fake, British accent with the word *wardrobe* that didn't sound great. It was like a southern cowboy met a South African. "Plus, I already informed Mikey you were taking a vacation. So, we are cleared for take-off." She boasted.

Glaring, I ground my teeth, while asking, "How did you manage my passport?" I could ignore the other stuff for now, but the passport worried me the most because you need a photo ID, birth certificate, and a social security number.

Bridget's eyes widened as she answered, "I borrowed your birth certificate and social security card. I used a picture I printed from my phone." Un-freaking-believable!

I screamed, "You did what?!" I couldn't believe my best friend. Yeah, she figured it out but it just ain't right taking off with other people's personal identification. It went beyond stealing and theft it was... it was.... Oh, I don't know what it was, but it's just wrong!

"I only borrowed them. I put them right back, so you didn't know. Besides, if I hadn't you'd never have done it yourself. If you think of it this way, you always said you felt your soulmate lived in England. Now we can figure out if your gut is right." She tried to be brave, and persuade me from being angry. Bananas, all in a ham basket, she succeeded! I have never been one to stay mad for long, not even when my low-life brother, Jared, stole from my bank account.

"Fine, I will go, but I am still mad at you," I said folding my arms, plopping down on our overstuffed, tan pleather couch. I tried faking my anger, but inside I couldn't help but be secretly thrilled. After all, I was going to be fulfilling an item on my bucket list.

Bridget rounded the card table, jumped on me and gave me a hug so tight that the air came out in one big whoosh. Releasing me from her death grip she bounced repeating, "Thank you! Thank you! Thank you!" She got out her thank you's before she continued, "Oh my gawd, we have to get ready for our trip. You need a whole new makeover! I am talking highlights, new nails, a pedicure, a push-up bra, high heels! Oh, and a totally cute luggage set! Girl, the one you have is in a sad sorry state!"

"Bridge, we can't afford that. Neither of us have that kind of cash to just splurge."

She jumped to her feet and walked to her room saying, "Let me handle that." I didn't even bother to respond to her enthusiasm and excitement. She'd call me a killjoy. I didn't mean to be a killjoy, but I was a realist. I found nothing wrong with being realistic. Shaking my head, I flopped it onto the back of the couch, and stared at the ceiling, before I leaned forward. With a groan, I stood up, and made my way to the card table to finish packing up the game.

We spent the rest of the evening traveling from one store to another because no store had everything she wanted. After going to what felt like fifty stores, we finally had everything Bridget thought we needed. I didn't think we needed to bring twenty different face creams or twelve different eyeshadow palettes.

Bridget had completely overspent, with no way to cover the amount. She was a hairdresser, and I, a housekeeper. I had made several investments, but my brother kept stealing what little surplus I made. To save money, she would add highlights to my hair and dye her own. Then, we would wax our legs, while we watched *Mamma Mia!*, ate Rocky Road Ice Cream and fell asleep during *Into the Woods*.

The following morning, we rushed around trying to pack everything. I packed only the essentials and helped Bridget pack everything we bought last evening. Shortly before noon, I had the strangest urge to make sure I packed my corset.

Our prearranged ride showed up right on time and an intimidating guy ushered us to the limousine. His name was Tod and built similar to "The Rock" only with a military buzz cut, and the personality of Sam in *New Moon*. The name Tod didn't seem to fit him. He felt more like a Ranger, or a Rocky. Either way, he gave me the heebie-jeebies. In a thick Greek accent, he asked, "Why do you need all this luggage?"

"Because we need to be able to make ourselves look fabulous at all times... duh! You never know if we'll get to meet any hunky guys, like you big boy...." Bridget flirted, "and we must have these suitcases to look our best." She batted her eyes, for an extra effect.

He grunted, "Get in the Limo. We have a deadline to keep." *This guy hustling us into the limo is taking us to the airport?* Bridget didn't seem perturbed being rebuffed by him, thinking *he's gay.* Honestly, he was not into high-maintenance girls like her. Bridget didn't understand what's wrong with being high-maintenance, but I got it, being on the opposite end of the maintenance graph. Give me a pair of sweatpants, a tank top, and a corner to read or write, and I am a happy camper.

Bridget wasn't as sensitive as me and found nothing wrong with being rushed off. However, my gut gave a nasty twinge as we seated ourselves. This sensation *always* foretold something horrid would happen.

Despite the dreadful feelings Tod gave me, he drove a spectacular limo. The light grey, stretch, SUV limo had a door which opened in the middle and inside could hold twenty people. Inside, three benches sat zigzag across from one another, with a mini-bar and a refrigerator sitting between them. I didn't get to enjoy much of the ride because I felt the need to keep a close eye on Bridget. She kept procuring alcohol from the mini-bar like a kid in a candy store and I didn't want to watch her get carried through the airport. The scene would be a little unsightly and awkward.

Before I knew it, we arrived at our destination. Tod rushed us out of the limo and through the airport. We didn't stop at the security section. Oddly enough, the guard let us skip the line and pass through, while all the other people flying acted like this happened all the time. It made no sense. Since 9/11, they had been implementing a strict security policy. Confused, I asked, "Why are we not going through security properly?"

"You are on a private plane and it is not needed." Tod acted like I was some kind of stupid lamb caught in a flood.

"But...?"

"Just keep moving," he growled, like a wild animal.

"We are trying! But you are going too fast! I am in heels you know." Bridget complained.

"Then, you should not have worn them." Tod replied.

"But they're cute." She pouted.

He got annoyed at this and paused long enough to pick Bridget up like a caveman. Then, he snapped at me, "Keep moving!" I didn't think I liked him much. Bridget held a Cheshire grin as she hung over his shoulder. Only she could find this type of treatment entertaining.

As we reached our charter, I couldn't help but get this strong sensation of dread the closer we got to the stairs of the plane. I couldn't listen to my intuition because Tod left me with no chance of changing course. As he continued my forward momentum, he directed me up the steps to our flight. Halfway up the short staircase, my gut demanded me to escape, saying the trip was a huge mistake.

Instinct had me wanting to flee and head back home, but Tod stood right behind me. He prevented my escape and instead waited for me to board the plane. When I didn't move, he barked, "Keep moving!"

I tried to speak my fears, but the more I kept trying to talk, the more air I lost. Soon, I lost consciousness. The moment I entered dreamland, I found myself stepping out of a limo, different than the one we traveled in to the airport. It was the type seen in the movies containing a diplomat. The limo had flags on it, but they weren't typical. They resembled the British flag only the red was black, the blue was a blood red, and the white was more of an ivory color. In the middle was an odd crest that sported a gray bat. The bat held a dark silver shield over what would be its body. The shield hung in the bat's mouth, as two fangs pierced it, and three small blood drops fell from the left fang. Seeing those flags made my heart beat pick up at a startling rate, forcing me awake.

I woke up in alarm and found everything blurry. Everything was fuzzy, not just my eyes, but hearing too. After a few seconds, things started to come into focus. I found myself staring at a worried looking guy, who was dabbing a wet cloth to my forehead. I didn't understand why he was worried, until he brought the cloth away and I saw blood, my blood. My heart picked up and I could feel my stomach wanting to empty everything inside of it. To keep everything where it should be, I focused more on the guy tending to my wounds. He had auburn hair, styled short and slick. His eyes were a green/brown hazel, his skin pale white, and his nose flared at a rather fast rate. It was like he smelled something he liked or didn't like.

I hadn't realized I'd sat up until the guy pushed me back down. I felt like a child, sick in bed. "Hey, relax! You fainted and have been out for quite some time," he said in an Irish brogue as he soaked the wet cloth, rung it out and dabbed my forehead again. "We tried to ask your friend if you fainted often, but she said you are afraid of heights. I believe you frightened her. We gave her some wine… umm, a few glasses of wine. She passed out in a pile of laughter. It was hilarious!"

Looking around confused, I inquired, "Where's Tod?"

"He was only to get you both on the plane. I would guess he is at home by now." He answered before asking, "Do you faint often?"

Staring at him, I replied, "Bridget is right. I get freaked out about heights. But that isn't why I fainted. The last thing I remember was getting this gut-wrenching feeling of terror, telling me to turn around and run. With no way to escape, my terror surged, and my body did the only thing it could. Sadly, I fainted."

His eyebrows furrowed together, "Your gut made you faint?"

I sighed, "Well, yes my gut told me not to get on this plane. I felt the unexplainable need to just go home or something awful will happen, but I couldn't flee anywhere."

He stood abruptly, looking very sad. "I am glad you are doing better. I should get back to work, now." He walked away briskly before I could say a single word.

CHAPTER 2

The Scary Car Ride

The flight was quiet and strange. I noticed that the plane was smaller than I expected. There were two, black, leather loveseats and two matching leather chairs. The chairs faced one another and held an anchored table between them. At the far end was a hallway lined with fold-out seating, for the attendants, and led to a bathroom. The entire plane held a chess color scheme. The furniture was black, while the walls were white, and the carpet had a checkered black-and-white pattern.

Occasionally, one of the four flight attendants would walk by, asking if I wanted anything to eat or drink or how they could make me comfortable. They seemed frightened of me, but I didn't think I was that horrifying. People always told me I was too nice for my own good. I asked a flight attendant, "What did I do wrong?" They ignored me and went on with their business. It was getting on my last nerve. *What was their problem? I didn't bite anybody as far as I could remember.* When we got ready to land, the pilot came over the intercom, saying, "Fasten your seatbelts for our descent."

All the workers on the plane buckled themselves up and didn't even bother to make sure Bridget or I were buckled. Buckling was the first thing I did after waking up, but Bridget slept away on the loveseat. I was raving mad at the lack of professionalism at this point. Unbuckling myself, I hopped over to the black loveseat a little way up from me. As I moved, several of the flight attendants yelled at me to get seated. I didn't listen, and instead kept making my way to my sleeping friend. I tried to sit her up and buckle her, but that didn't go over well as she had slapped me. Giving up, I lifted her head so I could sit and fastened myself up. I laid her head on my lap and became her human seat belt. I hoped this kept her from falling. Not that she'd care, since she was snoring up a storm.

As the jet descended toward earth, we hit turbulence. This caused my blood pressure to spike and to calm myself, I looked at my surroundings. I got an uncomfortable feeling, like I was being stared at. Looking towards the hallway, I found eight pairs of eyes staring at me. Six pairs of eyes stared as if I was a demon who had come to destroy their lives. One pair belonged to the man I woke up to, and when our eyes locked he quickly focused, in embarrassment, on his feet because he got caught. This made me wonder what was actually going on.

My body jerked to the right as we touched ground. Instinctively, my arms tightened around Bridget who mumbled, "No Bobo, not right now." Great! In her drunken stupor she thought I was one of her boy-toys.

After landing, I went to grab our bags, but the embarrassed steward, who I silently referred to as Mr. Weirdo, had already picked them up. He handed the bags to a short, blonde, young looking lady. He then returned to pick Bridget up and walked off the plane. I followed him into darkness. My annoyance had been building from all of the silent treatment on the plane. It increased with the inability to see where I was going. I kept bumping into Mr. Weirdo on my descent.

Eventually, we reached the ground and made our way to what would be our next ride. An outline of a man held open the limo door. As Bridget was still sleeping off her alcohol induced slumber, Mr. Weirdo tossed her into the vehicle like a bag of lion chow. I wanted to say, *how rude* but kept my mouth shut. I pushed Bridget's feet to the floor as I climbed in and sat her up-right. As I buckled Bridget in before myself, I heard Mr. Weirdo talking to the mystery man holding the door.

"Clarence, are you sure?" the unknown man whispered, in a British accent, to Mr. Weirdo. Finally! I knew his name. I am not sure why I hadn't looked for a name tag before, but I think my gut overpowered my common sense.

"Balin, I am certain. She told me on the plane she felt…" Clarence stated urgently, his words cut off, as Balin shut the door. I wondered *what are they all twitterpated about?*

A few minutes later, Balin got in the driver's seat. Rolling down the window, separating us, he said nervously, "We will be at our destination in about two hours. If you need to stop and stretch, roll this window down to let me know." I nodded my head, not sure what else to say. He mumbled something as he rolled the window up. I didn't understand what was going on, but I had a strong feeling of terror, that told me to walk as if I were on a frozen river.

Soon we were on our way. Like always, I fell asleep. This was a habit I hadn't grown out of from childhood. My dad said the motion of the vehicle had this calming effect on me that sent me to the moon. The odd thing about this was if I was the one driving, I could stay awake.

I slipped off into space, where I wished I hadn't gone. I was immediately running through a forest, when I tripped. Horrified by the fall, I scrambled to my feet, where I came face-to-face with a woman, who held an old chunky build. She looked as people do when they get old. When their whole body shifts and things start to sag. Places they liked shriveled and moved to the places they wished would go away. She had a small chest, medium thick arms with chicken flaps, a thick middle, wide hips, and legs that appeared to be retaining water. She had salt and pepper hair, jet-black eyes, and stood shorter than me, by four maybe five inches. The sight of her terrified me and I didn't even know the old bitty.

Whoever she was, she looked pissed off. Suddenly, she grabbed my arms in a firm grasp. It was so tight, it hurt. Naturally, I tried to pull free only to make the pain worse. Her hold hardened and in an angry French accent, she shrieked, "Leave this place! Do not go to the Prince's Castle! It is almost over; his punishment must continue. He must die, or your friend will die!"

I struggled to get away, when the forest vanished and changed to some handsomely dressed man holding Bridget. Bridget fell from the man's arms and landed at his feet. The man had blood running from his lips. Terror froze me because the scene reminded me of something from my pre-teens. I wanted to run to Bridget to see if she was alive. However, I remained stuck in my place, by both my fear and the old bitty, who wouldn't let me go.

I screamed Bridget's name, but no sound came out. I heard the old hag laugh, "See, your friend will die first, then you. All thanks to that Prince. Turn back now!"

The grasp of the old hag left and I ran towards Bridget, only to have her disappear. Panic filled me and I started shouting her name. I didn't understand what was happening. A sound came from behind me. As I spun around, I stared into deep, blood-red eyes that looked demonic. The sight of this caused me to scream and jerk myself awake.

The vehicle came to a stop and Balin rolled down the dividing window, "Are you all right Miss?"

Holding my hand over my heart and waiting for it to stop pounding, I stuttered, "Y-yes I fell a-asleep and had a b-bad dream is a-all. I sometimes talk in my sleep. Or r-rather I do everything you do in your a-awake state while asleep. It's not so un-unusual for me."

He frowned saying, "That is unusual. Do you suffer from a mental disorder?"

Used to the response, I replied, "For most people, I suppose yes it would be, but I hold back a lot of my feelings and they manifest while I am asleep."

"I will tell the Masters and the servants about your sleeping habits, Miss," He said turning off the ignition and climbing out of the limo.

As I automatically opened my door, I recovered from the surprise of the use of nineteenth century terms that felt out of place in today's society. Stepping from the limo, I spotted Balin, who looked a lot taller than anticipated. Rounding the back-end of the vehicle, he didn't look too happy about something. His hair was dark brown, and he had dark blue eyes. His fair skin enveloped his medium build. I wondered *is being tall and handsome an epidemic around here?*

Balin came and held the door open wider for another gentleman, who just materialized out of nowhere. I stepped away from the limo, so the young man could wrangle Bridget out. While he worked on getting Bridget, Balin, whose angry expression never left, said, "Miss, the next time you feel the need to open your own door, do not!"

Stunned, but not into speechlessness, I replied, "Sorry! It was just out of habit. I am so used to doing it on my own I didn't give it much thought." Balin didn't say a word and the young man finally got a good grip on Bridget's sleeping form. The young man, who carried Bridget like a bride, had flaming red hair. I couldn't see much else, other than him being taller than me and gangly thin. I felt like he needed a good hearty meal, but that was just my nurturing side coming out. I couldn't help wondering how he could carry Bridget. I know for a fact she is not a light person when passed out. She becomes the phrase "dead weight" in the literal sense and I swear she weighed as much as an elephant.

At the sound of the vehicle door closing, I jumped. I spun to look where the sound had originated, only to feel Balin whisk by, brushing my shoulder. I was about to snap at Balin's crude behavior, but that was no longer my concern. My eyes caught the front of the British limo. It was identical to my dream. Right down to the flags. My heartbeat picked up speed and I was certain I turned a few shades whiter. My breathing hitched, and I had a hard time catching it. Not wanting to pass out yet again, I closed my eyes and turned away because I feared what I might see or dream next. I could feel something dreadful was coming. I didn't know what or when it would happen. It was really starting to freak me out.

Opening my eyes, I stared at a huge castle and thought to myself, *WOW! This place is huge*! I had only seen castles in movies or pictures. This, in person, was holy-crow beautiful! It looked like a cross between Mr. Darcy's home from *Pride and Prejudice* and the stereotypical castle used in movies.

The limo parked in a wide-open courtyard, with a wooden-plank drawbridge, leading up to the castle. On the other side of the bridge, stood a *Rocky*-like staircase that led up to the main entrance, where a giant double-door stood. I couldn't help but wonder *had a giant ever gone through those doors?* The front stood nearly six stories tall. The walls stretched five semi-truck lengths on either side, ending with a bastion tower similar to Rapunzel in *Tangled*. It looked like there was an even bigger and fatter tower standing right in the middle of the castle. It made me feel insignificant. I couldn't understand why somebody who owned a place like this, would hold a writing contest, giving winners a free trip for two to their own home. It felt like this was all a publicity stunt or they had an ulterior motive.

Looking at this place, I knew I didn't need my gut to tell me something was amiss. It felt like a death sentence, as if all the horror that had taken place oozed out from the limestone blocks and needed to be purged of its sins. The dark, ominous clouds looming above foretold a tale as old as time. Noticing Balin and the young redhead were nearly to the gigantic door I raced to catch-up. Entering the massive castle gasping for air, Balin stated, "Wait here. I shall get the young Master."

Balin left in a hurry. Hands on my knees, I tried to catch my breath, as I stood next to the redhead still toting an unconscious Bridget. My breathing returned to normal as I absorbed the interior. The walls in the entryway had cabin-like wood paneling that was stained a cherry red.

Anticipating stone, I found the paneling to be an unexpected choice for a castle. Twin staircases went up on either side of the entryway. At the top, I could barely see three passageways that led in different directions. On the right and left side of the entryway were hidden hallways, leading to antechambers. A wide, double-door filled the center void of the staircases. The doors and frame matched the paneling. Looking up at the ceiling, a huge crystal chandelier hung. Instead of glowing light bulbs, it held bright white candles. I thought to myself, *I would never want the job of having to light, blow out, and replace those candles.*

Getting curious about the redhead's name, I stared at the old oil paintings. I finally dared to ask, "So... what is your name?" I felt it was the polite thing to do since he was holding my best friend. I was surprised he hadn't dropped to his knees from all of her dead weight.

Glancing at him, he didn't turn my way, and he seemed like he almost didn't want to answer. After a few minutes, he mumbled in a Scottish accent, "Leon." It was so quiet, I almost didn't even hear him. It was Deja-vu. The plane ride all over again. I decided to just wait and absorb the peacefulness of the beautiful entryway.

CHAPTER 3

The Witch

I sat with my eyes closed, remembering my twin soul. *The simplest things made her laugh and the sound was like a soft, gentle breeze moving through a willow branch. Her eyes were the color of a dark stormy day, and her hair was the soft color of the sun. She had angel kisses along her nose and cheek. Her body was…* My fantasizing was interrupted when Balin coughed. Balin was the Shade Advisor and has spent most of his time keeping tabs on me. He found me again in a secret spot, tucked way up on the top floor of our four-story library. I spend some of my day in this darkened spot sitting, hidden away, pining for my twin soul. I dreamt of her as she was alive. Even reliving the nightmare of her death and my curse, I did not blame her. It had not been her fault. It had been the bloody witch's fault! She was the one who took everything from me.

Fists clenched, I snarled, "Balin, unless you have something vitally important to tell me, you best bugger off!" Balin stood frozen. All I wanted was to bask in my memories of my beloved Isadora. I could have given two-craps-less about whatever Balin wanted because in a few short weeks I would finally be with my twin soul. When he did not leave, I snapped, "Can you not see I am trying to meditate here, Balin? I could not care less about whatever the trivial problem, maybe. You can just take the problem to my parents. After all they are still the king and queen."

My own parents had given up on me, along with the servants. My parents had been trying to have another son and had been unsuccessful. I was a fluke because our kind had been having problems with conception. The King and Queen had wished to retire, or die. Since I was their only child, they could not do so without another living heir to pass on the Shade Kingdom. Everyone felt I should be doing anything I could to end my curse, however, I knew the end was fast approaching and I looked forward to seeing my soulmate again.

Balin took a deep breath, "Athelstan, this is not a Shade problem. This is your problem."

I could feel the blood rush into my eyes. Moving from my seated position I growled, "You know the proper way to address me. My parents may have passed me over for the next in line to my cousin Dayton. However, I am still a royal until my death. You best not be forgetting that, nor your station!"

"Please, forgive me your highness, but there is a colossal problem with the contest winners." He bowed his head showing his respect towards my position.

As my anger dropped and the blood left my eyes, I asked, "What did the winner bring? Her boyfriend? Husband? Significant other?"

"Well, no. Nothing like that your Majesty. Bridget Scott has brought a female friend."

"Then, I fail to see a problem, Balin. If my memory serves me right, I never asked for another contest. My parents went behind my back running this whole fiasco. You know I would have never picked the United States out of all the countries in the world. Half of the mortals from the new colonies are poor, weak and whiny. The other half are bitchy, money-grubbing, power-hungry wenches who do not last long, and their blood tastes foul, like it has an unknown toxin in it."

"Yes, your Highness. You have said this all before. However, this goes beyond what you think and feel about the Americans."

Agitated, I walked away. It was not like anyone knew, beside my parents, that I found and lost my other half. All everyone seemed to care about was breaking the spell, my curse. I have been trapped in this castle for four hundred and seventy-four years and will soon be six hundred years old. This was too much time to live without one's twin soul. Most Cimmerians would have lost their wits, but I have managed to keep mine, somehow.

I have often wondered, *Is the reason I have kept my sanity the spell… or my inner strength?* The thought of my immortality coming to an end, brought me great joy, for once in many years. I was not going to let anything or anyone get in my way. Least of all, this last pathetic attempt by my parents to end the curse, nor these stupid mortals that had been lured into my prison.

We were halfway down the hallway when Balin broke up the silence, by blurting, "The winner brought a witch with her, sir." This stopped me dead in my tracks. Spinning around, quicker than he could blink, I let out a low growl. Ever since my curse, I had loathed all witches or magic wielders. He took four steps back the moment he saw my eyes fill with blood and my fangs drop.

It was a good decision because I had the urge to drain someone. The Cimmerian Shade people did not need to drink blood as was told by the myths and legends. We only needed blood if we were extremely pissed off, causing our blood to boil, or during the three nights of the new moon. Clenching my fists and closing my eyes, I yelled, instead of draining, "Miss Scott's brought a what! How do you know that she is a witch?!"

"Your Highness, while they were being loaded into the family car, Clarence informed me Miss Scott's companion fainted as she was boarding the private jet. He said when Miss Holmes woke up, she told him she felt something dreadful would happen if she got on the plane. She also disclosed to him it was a gut feeling and her gut was never wrong."

Opening my eyes, I looked Balin over deliberating on the new information. Grinding my teeth, I snapped, "That does not mean she is a witch! However, it does not mean she is not one either. I will just avoid her and focus my attention on the actual contest winner." I figured this would appease him, but I had other ideas.

With a sad undertone, he replied, "It may be for the best, sir. In the meantime, we will have to pray that Miss Scott is the one."

I spun back around, trying to lower my rage, before meeting Miss Scott and her friend. *We could not let them learn about the Cimmerians too soon. It would ruin all my fun in torturing them.* I enjoyed playing with my food because it had become the only way for me to endure my long captivity.

Continuing towards the entrance hall, neither of us said another word. I knew Balin was big on prayers. His belief in it working astonished me. I did not believe praying worked. If he prayed for me, it would have been a big waste of his time. There was no way in heaven or hell I would fall in love with any mortal. Mortals were fragile, insubstantial beings, who craved longevity and took simple pleasures for granted. My parents claimed it was my distaste of mortals that had stopped any emotions from blooming. The fact I was a Cimmerian Shade and needed blood to survive, was a small role in my choices. I much preferred my blood fresh and not from a bottle, which had become customary for the Cimmerians. This was why mortals never lasted long around me and always returned in a casket. As we rounded the last corner, I found myself at the top of the landing staring down at my unwanted guests.

I did not descend the stairs right away because I saw one was sleeping and the other looked bored. It was rather intriguing. The one that slept in Leon's arms had a tan skin tone. She was obviously a fan of the sun and of dying her hair blonde. I could smell the dye from up here and it stank like cat urine. Her eyebrow color showed me she was a natural brunette. The malodor of the dye masked the scent of her blood type, which was a delightful A negative. I did not care for blondes, nor girls who dyed their hair. The ladies, in this time, who worked hard to maintain a certain look were exceedingly high maintenance. I much preferred a more natural look on my women and knew she would be a challenge.

The girl who looked bored, stood about five foot, three inches tall. She looked more than well fed. Her hair was a medium brown, but had blonde highlights, which smelled most recent. She had green/brown eyes, a rather broad nose, rosy cheeks, and plump lips. I wondered, *is she the witch?* I let out a low growl, which I did not think any mortal could hear. The second the sound escaped from my throat, her head popped up in my direction. As our eyes locked, my frozen heart felt warm. Something stirred within me, giving life once again to the fractured organ. I did not like the sensation and knew she was someone I should avoid at all costs during the duration of her stay.

Starting down the stairs, our eyes remained locked through my descent as if we were both unable to look away. This perturbed me, as the overwhelming urge to get closer to her had me looking into her mind. I found her mind very difficult to break because her thoughts had a steel wall in front of them. Witches did not usually block our mind-reading abilities, nor wanted to. They found it much easier to let us in, as it allowed them to read our thoughts as well.

Reaching the bottom of the stairs, I decided two things: First, I liked neither girl. The second was this wench was a powerful being. I needed to figure out what kind of creature she was and when I did, I would destroy her.

It bothered me not being able to read a mortal's mind; it made things less entertaining because I did not know how to irritate her whenever she annoyed me. I got the sense that this girl would annoy me quite often. Frowning, I began my rehearsed spiel, "Welcome to my wonderful home. My name is Athelstan Moren, but you can call me Stan. I hope you can feel at home in my lovely abode....

"Balin will escort you to your chambers to get settled in. Please come and join us for dinner, in the dining room, in about an hour. There should be a map of the Moren castle in your rooms to prevent you from losing your way." I mustered up what pleasantries I could, reminding myself of the surprises awaiting in their rooms.

"Thank you, Stan, for sharing your home. I will be down, but I don't think Bridge will be able to join us. Your stewards made the mistake of giving her wine and wine doesn't agree with her system. I don't believe she will be awake until sometime in the night or early morning," the wench mumbled, extending her hand for me to shake, adding, "Forgive me, I never told you my name. It's Nicole, Nicole Marie Holmes."

I was not about to shake Nicole's hand. After a few seconds, she realized this herself and lowered her extended limb. I bowed my head to her and left as quickly as I came in. I could not believe I was to spend my last remaining days with these two pompous mortals. They were by far the worst contestants to set foot in my home.

CHAPTER 4

The Chamber

After Stan made his insincere greeting, he refused to shake my hand by simply walking off. Balin finally joined us on the ground floor and politely said, "Shall I show you to your rooms?" Nodding my head in silence, I followed Balin up the right staircase, only to take an immediate right at the top. We went down a long corridor and up a small flight of stairs, then down another corridor, through a doorway and down a smaller flight of stairs. The whole way I felt as if I had stepped out of time, walking right into the movie of *A Kid in King Arthur's Court*.

All along the stone hallways, I found lit torches hanging every few feet with tables in between. The torches didn't look like those described in books or I had seen in the movies. They were like misshapen bats, whose mouths laid open to emit light. Some of the tables held candlesticks with red homemade candles. They looked like nothing I had seen before. The candlesticks looked like wolves, howling at the moon. Their howls held the candles while their bodies were coated with old candle wax.

As I contemplated, who could create such bizarre metal works or who'd have them in their home, I'd lost track of the path Balin made to our sleeping quarters. Before I knew it, we arrived in the hallway where the new rooms would become our home for the next few weeks.

The first door on the right, Balin told me, belonged to Bridget, while the first door to the left belonged to me. Leon took Bridget's sleeping form into her room as Balin opened my bedroom door. Walking in, Balin said, "All your luggage has been brought up and you will find new clothes in your wardrobe. There should be enough for your whole stay." Walking in, I found myself in a room, lit dimly by candlelight, as was the rest of the castle. On the way to this temporary bedroom, I didn't spot one bulb, or outlet, nor light switch. *Had they not heard of electricity? After all, it was the best invention since the corset.* Turning to ask, "Why only candles?" I found myself alone. *Alrighty then, I will have to ask later.*

Spinning back to my interim accommodations, I absorbed the new environment. The room was pretty big, being twenty-three feet long, by thirty feet wide, by fifteen feet high. To my left rested a beautiful, old, dark colored, four-poster-bed with thick maroon curtains all around. It had reminded me of a renaissance movie. The bed was done up in a blood red and ivory flower pattern. It was something I wouldn't have gone for because I didn't really find flowery stuff appealing.

Across from the door, on the far wall, rested a mystery door. Sitting next to the mystery door stood a large wooden vanity. The vanity held all kinds of jewelry that looked custom made and very old. Standing across from the poster bed lay rooted a large cabinet with a very intricate design. The intricate carving was of fish and whales in waves. The imagery was rather strange as it appeared to be moving. I couldn't help but think, *This place is odd with bats for torches, wolves for candlestick holders, and now sea life carved into wood? At least they kept to the same color scheme and didn't have everything mismatched.* Resting in the middle of the room, on top of a very old rug, sat an old fainting couch. I was not exactly sure how old the couch was, but it had a faded pink fabric that at one time may have been a darker shade of red.

After investigating my new abode's decor, I decided it was time to unpack. Someone had laid my three bags on the floor at the end of my new bed, haphazardly. *I guess it was a good thing I didn't have anything breakable in them.* Picking the bags up, I set them on the bed. I started with the pink camo carry-on, pulling out my shampoo, conditioner, and body soap setting them down on the mattress. Then, I pulled out a bottle of shaving cream and oil, my *Venus* razor, hair brush, and a comb. I laid them all out before I began to dig through the bag once again. I took out a bottle of hair gel, a can of hairspray, my small bag of scrunchies, other hair bands, hair pins, hair clips, and a hair necklace which sits on top of your head, instead of your neck. It's a rather beautiful piece and I didn't get to wear it too often. I brought it in the off chance I got to wear it for something while we were here.

After I emptied my bag, I went to put the toiletries in the bathroom. Looking around I wasn't sure where it was. *I'll see if the mystery door leads me to a washroom. If it does, then this would be a suite and that would be plain sweet. If it doesn't, I will need to find someone and ask them. Well, I will hope the door leads me into a restroom.*

Opening the door, I found myself in another dimly lit room, but was surprised that this one actually had a window in it. It was a little bit brighter, but not by much. I was thrilled to find the bathroom, but it didn't look like it had any running water, nor did it have a toilet. It did have a very old, rich, fancy, renaissance tub with claw feet, which I looked forward to using.

On the back wall, was a table that had a bunch of different sized bottles. Across from the table, to the right as you walked in, was a small counter that held a big ceramic bowl. The basin was already filled with water. There were two, neatly folded washcloths lying on either side of the bowl. I was seriously beginning to wonder, *How am I going to potty without a toilet?*

Deciding to worry about the potty issue later, I walked over to the ornate bottles on the table. They screamed at me to be opened and my curiosity got the better of me. The bottles on either end smelled like someone died in them, while the others held a more pleasant aroma. The one in the middle smelled the best. It smelled like milk and honey and I wanted to drink it all up. I had to restrain myself from doing that as I was pretty sure the bottles were filled with some kind of soap. As I noticed a blood red, sample sized bottle labeled "A-," a door opened on my left, which startled me. I didn't even know it was there because it blended in so well with the wall.

In walked a petite girl with red hair, blue eyes, flushed cheeks, and a dark complexion. She couldn't have been any older than fifteen or sixteen and she carried a rather large jug that was half her size. I walked quickly over to her and tried to help, by grabbing ahold of the jug, saying, "Here, let me help you."

"Oh, no Miss, I can do it. It is my job after all," she replied sweetly and nervously in a British accent.

"Oh, it's no problem, I do housekeeping for a living, too. You can call me Nicole. No 'Miss' please."

The girl smiled as she caved, letting me help her walk the large jug over to a corner, to the right of the counter. After she fixed the jug to sit perfectly, she stood up looking confused and asked, "Is there something you need Miss?"

I can see we were going to have problems. Sighing, I implored, "Really! Call me Nicole or Nicki and the only thing I need to know is where the toilet might be?"

She looked at me baffled, "Miss, I am not quite sure what a toilet is."

Staring at her, I tried to think of a way to explain a toilet. Thinking hard, I tried to come up with other terms. Finally, I tried to explain, "Well it's a John, Loo …ummm… you know the thing you use to go…ummm."

"Oh, yes! I know what you mean now. We do not have any of those here." *They don't have any toilets here?* "There are only chamber pots for the rooms and then there is an outhouse, which is about a half mile away from the house," she said, as if preparing for me to start yelling. *Why would she be cowering over the toilet issue, or the lack thereof? It is not as though she is responsible for the amenities.*

I sighed, before asking, "A chamber pot? So, this place has no indoor plumbing?" She nodded her head, apologetically. "I guess from the candles, there is also no electricity as well? Fabulous!" I paused long enough to calm myself, before saying, "This is a rather big chamber pot. I didn't know they made them this big. I do love the midnight blue with gold swirl inlay, though." I mean the beast came up to my thigh, but I found it unusually stunning.

She laughed, then said, "Sorry, Miss. It is a bit medieval here. The chamber pot is large and changed every other day, instead of small and needing changed every few hours. There is electricity, however, it only powers one place in the castle and that is the kitchen."

"Ok, will I be able to find the kitchen on the map Stan said would be in my room? Would it be possible to use an outlet, in case I need to charge my phone or laptop?" She nodded her head vigorously and started to leave, but before she left wholly I asked, "What if I need to bathe? How do I get the water?"

"I will bring water in for you to bathe, once a week, and bring in fresh water for your basin, every day, for you to get freshened up," she answered before bowing and quickly leaving. *Once a week? I usually take a shower every two days. How on earth does one get clean by only freshening up? Bridget is not going to like this. She takes a shower every day and sometimes three times a day! I will be hiding when she finds out about the lack of modern bathroom conveniences.*

CHAPTER 5

The Yellow Gown

Stocking the bathroom and unpacking my other bags only took me a few minutes, however, I spent a while figuring out what Balin meant by wardrobe. What I thought to be a cabinet with intricate carvings, ended up being the wardrobe he spoke of. I was taken by surprise at the many gowns, within the wooden box, because they seemed to be straight out of a Shakespeare play. *Do they really expect me to wear such things? What kind of twisted humor do these people have? It's a good thing I decided to bring my corset, after all. If they think I'm going to wear one of those dresses, with the whale bone corset resting at the bottom of the wardrobe, they're insane. I much prefer to breathe pleasantly, thank you very much.*

Trying to get a better view of the gowns and failing miserably, due to weak arm muscles and an overstuffed wardrobe, the door to my room opened, startling me. As I yelped and whirled around, I spotted a blonde girl about my height, standing in the doorway. The girl's eyes went straight to the floor, as she did a curtsy. Before her face moved from view, I noticed the guilty expression in her light blue eyes and a grimace on her pink lips. Her eyes remained glued to the floor as she straightened and said in a Dutch accent, "I am here, Miss, to help you get ready for dinner."

Help me get ready for dinner? Wait! Wouldn't it be lunch time? It's about noon or maybe one right now. Looking down at my clothes I ask, "What's wrong with what I have on?"

Her eyes snapped up horrified and confused, "I am here to see that you are properly dressed to sit at the table with the masters, Miss. I mean no disrespect to your clothing choices, however, how can you go around dressing as a man? It is quite improper, Miss."

I stared at her blankly. *Dressing as a man... improper? It would have been considered indecent about seventy-five years ago, but today it was more common. Alright, I will bite and play along. I do enjoy me a good ren-fair,* "Ok then, make me look proper for the Duke and Duchess. But, if I am to wear one of those gowns, I insist in wearing my own corset. I much prefer being able to breathe normally."

She stared at me blankly, before replying, "You are most unusual; most girls these days fight me and the other maids, about having to dress of old and having to use the chamber pots." She realized she said something she shouldn't have and stared at the floor once more saying, "Miss, please disregard what I just said."

I laughed and turned back towards the wardrobe saying, "Of course, I won't say a word. Besides, I am not like most girls and pride myself on that. So... which one of these will you squeeze me into then?" Scanning over the sliver of the gowns I could see, I found a lot of red and black. *I ain't going to complain because I love red, but there are also greens and yellows mixed in with the other dresses and that concerns me. Yellow completely washes me out and green should only be found on a tree.*

The girl walked up next to me and pulled out a yellow dress saying, "You will wear this one, Miss." She took the heavy dress out as if it was nothing and laid it on the fainting couch. The hideous thing was an almost dark yellow and had a light brown, almost cream-colored floral design on the bottom of the skirt. The sleeves were puffy at the shoulders and got slimmer as they went down the arm coming to a point on the hand. I knew the look on my face was horror as I thought, *This gown is going to make me look like death warmed over.*

Looking at the gown, I begged, "Must I wear the yellow one? Yellow makes me look dead and gross."

"I am sorry Miss, but it is the Master's favorite color and I was told to make sure you wear this specific gown," she said as she went through the vanity drawers.

"I'm not here to appease your Master. I am here because my friend...." I paused because it didn't rightly matter why. "Alright fine! Let's get that hideous thing on and get lunch over with, so that I can strip it off as quickly as possible," I finished.

"Miss, I am confused," she stated, looking much like a dog does when they hear a sound they don't understand. The, "huh," motion that's really cute and could be watched all day long. She made that motion and it was the first time I'd seen a person do that before.

I sighed, "It's alright. It is confusing to me as well. But can you do me a favor?" She nodded, "Please stop calling me Miss! My name is Nicole and I do not like the 'Miss' as it makes me feel like I am back in school."

"I am sorry Miss... sorry Nicole. I will make sure you are called by your name from now on."

"Thank you, but you know it would be easier if I knew your name. Unless you want me to call you, Hey You?" I asked.

"My name is Christa Forster," she giggled and did another curtsy.

It took us a while to get me into the ugly dress. Once I had the thing on, I understood why people back in the day both stayed fit and needed someone to dress them. It was a big production to get the dress on and it had to weigh about thirty pounds. *Good Lord, I hope to never have to get into another gown again!*

Once the gown was on, Christa gave me a once over to make sure it was on correctly. While she checked me over and fixed *my girls*, I stared at my reflection in the vanity mirror. *I look worse than death and that is pretty bad.* Broken from my thoughts of myself in the ugly yellow gown, Christa commented, "You know, you are right."

Confused, I tore my eyes away from the horrifying sight in the vanity and asked, "Right about what?" *What was I right about? Normally I am rarely ever wrong about things. Bridget is constantly telling me that I am an annoying know-it-all.*

Christa laughed, "You are right, yellow is not a good color on you. I will be sure to remove all the other yellow dresses in your wardrobe." Her laughter was contagious, and I started to laugh with her. After our giggle fit, she helped me with my hair. The way she pulled it all back, putting a bunch of bobby pins in, and letting some of the hair in the back fall freely, looked absolutely beautiful on me. It looked like one of the hair styles used in the old medieval movies. She then went into the wardrobe and pulled out a matching headdress. It held a stone in the center, the same shade of yellow as the dress, and was being held by off white lace. After she put it on, I felt like the Princess from *The Never Ending Story*. It made me feel like royalty.

As Christa straightened the head piece, so that the yellow gem sat center on my forehead she said, "Alright. It is about time for dinner and you are all ready to go."

"Oh, Good Lord!" I said exasperatingly, "I feel locked up tighter than a jukebox!" Christa laughed. I didn't find it too funny because I was being serious. Christa kept chuckling as she left the room, before I could even ask her how to find the dining hall. *I guess I'll have to find the dining hall myself. Now, where is that map?*

Sitting on the vanity stool, I opened drawers and started digging through them. Not finding the map there, I began searching the whole room, turning it into a war zone. Giving a frustrated shout at not being able to find the dumb map, I decided to put the room back in order.

As I placed the last bag at the foot of the bed, I found the map. It had been hiding under my suitcases and sitting directly in the middle of the king-sized bed. *Why is it when you really want to find something it's always in the last place you look?*

Walking over, I had to figure out a way to reach the map that rested in the center. Sitting in the dress was one thing; bending over was near impossible. Grabbing the luggage had been easier due to the bulkiness, but the map was a flat piece of paper. Determined, I pushed the hoop skirt backwards and tried to reach for the map, only to fall over onto the bed. I flopped my way into the middle, like a wet fish on dry land. I was pretty sure if anybody had been around, they would have laughed, which made me thankful to be alone. Once my finger touched the map, I scooted it closer to me and clutched it tightly.

Now, how do I get off the bed? Doing more fish impressions, I scooted my way off the bed, landing with a thud. Grabbing one of the bedposts, I was able to right myself. *Geez! That was a work out! I can barely breathe.* Catching my breath, I decided two things: Firstly, I might have loved the clothes from the Renaissance, but I much preferred simpler clothes. The second thing was, I would have to ask if there was a town nearby because I would not be able to survive much longer in these things… let alone for three weeks. If there was a town, I would be able to buy some full-length dresses that were far more comfortable.

Flipping the map around, I tried to figure out where I was on it, but it didn't have one of those "you are here" dots. It would have also been really helpful to know which way was up and down on the map. I decided to return to the hallway and trust my gut to get me back to the entryway.

CHAPTER 6

The Interesting Dinner

After a while, I felt like I was going in circles. My gut couldn't make up its mind as to which way it wanted me to go. *This must be how normal people feel, when they get turned around and lost. It's strange my gifts should fail me, in this place.* Eventually, I made it to the entrance and had to take a breather. Catching my breath, I pulled out the horrid map and found where I was. The map had poor penmanship and was hard to read. I finally figured out where I was to be for dinner, for which I was already late.

The dining hall entrance was literally right in front of me. Folding the map, I placed it in the only place I could, my corset. Then, I hurried towards the double doors. I took a couple of deep breaths before reaching for the handle. As I went to open the doors, they opened on their own, causing me to flinch and in this heavy gown it was strenuous.

Walking in tentatively, I looked around. *Surprise! Another dimly lit room.* The room was somewhat plain, in my opinion, when compared to the bat shaped torches and wolf candlestick holders flooding the hallways. There were no windows and the only source of light came from all the candles. The medieval, grey-stone room was very long and huge, and could double as a ballroom. The rectangular space had an extremely old, long, wooden table, sitting right smack dab in the middle. Hanging from the ceiling was three large, wooden chandeliers. I felt like I had been thrown back in time and was beginning to wonder if I was even still in the twenty-first century.

The large wooden table looked big enough to sit about seventy to eighty people, although it currently sat ten; four women and six men, who all sat at one end and stared right at me. Well almost all of them anyway, Stan was busy stuffing his face.

Stan sat at the head of the table, in all his smugness. *He is one, I'm not so sure I'm going to like too much.* Glancing over the faces sitting around the table, I found myself staring at a Fabio-like man sitting the farthest from Stan, on his right side. He had long, dark hair with baby blue eyes. His lips looked very kissable and lick-able with his medium build. He was the type of guy I had always dreamed of being with but knew he would never go for an ordinary girl like me. *I am a Disney geek with a little fat on the side. I have what my friends call a Faerie Tale syndrome because I dream of happily ever after. Well, somewhat, because no one lives happily ever after.*

"Glad to see you can finally join us for dinner," Mr. Fabio said, with an annoyed British undertone. He then switched to a sweetful grace, remembering he was a gentleman, "Sorry we had to start without you."

Surprised by the one-eighty flip, I said, "No, it's alright. I got lost because of this stupid map and I'm happy to have made it."

Balin walked over to an empty chair that sat right across from Mr. Fabio, who said, "Why not join us, then?" He gestured to the pulled-out chair in Balin's hands. As I walked over, all the men stood up, except for Stan who continued to eat and intensely watched me walk to my seat. They all sat down after I did and went back to staring at me in silence.

As Balin set a bowl of mystery soup in front of me, I asked, "Do I have something on my face?"

A brawny sized guy, with dark brown hair, sitting next to me, started to chuckle, "No, Ma'am it is your attire. It is uh..., different." Shaking his head in an attempt to remember his manners, he said in a Scottish accent, "Let me introduce myself. I am Knox and this...," He gestured to the girl who looked like a female version of himself, "is my twin sister, Kimberley."

Confused, I asked, "What is wrong with my clothes?" Then, I noticed that everyone at the table wore clothes from this time and not the middle ages.

The woman who sat on the other side of Kimberley, said in a Scottish accent, "No dear, there is nothing wrong with your dress, if you like that sort of thing. However, why are you wearing something so out of date?" My instincts told me this dark-haired woman had a mother's softness, but the way she sat with authority said her word was *the* law.

Before I responded to the woman, I looked directly at Stan, who chose that moment to stop eating and smiled slyly. "Umm... this is what the maid said I was to wear. Plus, the wardrobe in my room is filled with more dresses just like this one." Frowning down at the awful yellow dress,

I came to the conclusion that the sly smile on Stan's face meant the gowns were his idea. *He did it deliberately to irritate me! I am not going to give you the satisfaction of that.* With a smile on my face, I added, "I don't like this color, but I really do enjoy wearing it. It makes me feel like a princess."

The woman, along with the man sitting next to her, took on angry expressions and turned to look at Stan. The woman in a stern, yet gentle voice said, "Athelstan Kirkley Moren, what have we told you about having our old gowns placed in the contestant winner's wardrobes?" He didn't answer and very quietly ate a spoonful of mystery soup.

I couldn't help but wonder how many contests had been held and how many women had been here. Laughing, I said, "Ma'am, it's quite alright. I don't really mind wearing this for now, but I do hope that you can allow me, at some point, to buy my own clothing. I did bring some money and even though it may not buy much, it should be enough to get by on this trip."

She gave Stan a disappointed, motherly look before turning to me and apologized, "No dear. We will send one of the servants to shop for you. It is not safe for the two of you to leave the castle grounds. I am afraid you will have to wear the gowns in your wardrobe for a while."

I looked at her, shocked for a few moments, before I said, "I am fine with wearing this kind of stuff, however, Bridget won't like it too much. It's never been her thing. But, I don't think it will be that dangerous for me to leave the umm… grounds." *How could I possibly be in danger leaving their estate?*

Then, the man sitting next to her, who looked like a older version of Stan, looked at me with a very stern expression, and said in a British accent, "It is quite unsafe, young lady, for you to be by yourself off castle grounds. Therefore, please refrain from leaving unless escorted in a vehicle or by a bodyguard."

At that point, I felt very disheartened, "Then we aren't able to leave until the three weeks are up? With all due respect sir, I had hoped to go to London for a few days while I'm here. It's the only reason I came on this stupid trip with my friend in the first place. I may never get to come back to England again and I really wanted to see London."

Stan's mother looked rather surprised by my statement, as did everybody else at the table, including Stan. He shook it off quickly, casually taking a sip out of his wine glass saying in a British accent, "Well then, why come at all if you didn't want to be here in the first place?"

Looking down at my soup, which was very cold by now, I became horrified by the green contents and the odd, floating grey meat. I felt like they gave me a big bowl of vomit. The smell of it alone made me feel very queasy. Trying to focus on something else, I decided to answer, "I argued with Bridget on the matter, but she saw this as a great opportunity for me to go to the one place I've always wanted to see. She knows what coming to England means to me, but I never wanted to come here like this. I knew I would lose our disagreement when she put on her determined face and this meant no matter how much I argued, the subject was a moot point. Besides, she knows I have felt my soulmate lived here or on a coast line."

Stan laughed and said, "You think your soulmate is here? In Jolly Old England? Now that is priceless, because soulmates, Miss Holmes, *do not exist.*"

I was especially furious with him. *Who was he to say soulmates didn't exist? I firmly believed in soulmates and I knew I was going to find mine.* Snapping, "Says the guy who's grown up with everything at his beckon-call. But then again, what would a mere peasant like me rightfully know about anything that you, your highness, would know better. And furthermore, I bet you don't believe in anything that you don't know to be true or haven't seen with your own eyes. I would even wager you don't even believe in faeries, werewolves, witches, goblins, the loch ness monster, or even vampires."

He glared at me and growled, "What would a simpleton like you know about witches or vampires other than the shite mortals write in trivial books and movie scripts?!"

I stared at him with pure hatred flowing through my veins. As a rule, I didn't hate people. Hate was the opposite of love and was just as powerful. But for some reason, he had me loathing him into hatred. "I don't know much about vampires, but I also don't take all the crap that is written down as fact. Witchcraft, however, I have had my dealings with and I don't like it at all."

Mr. Fabio angrily asked, "You've dealt with witches?" He isn't so cute when angered.

With a groan I said, "Yes. It wasn't a pleasant encounter as the warlock was my boyfriend and his mother was a witch. They felt that I held a very strong, hidden power and wanted me to utilize it. I told them they were nuts, but they insisted I take part in their circle and learn the craft itself. I firmly believe that witchcraft can be both good and bad, however, it should never be messed with or taken lightly. They kept pushing me. I had no other choice but to end my relationship with him. I didn't want to, but he left me no choice when he wouldn't stop bugging me about learning. They ended up deciding since I wouldn't learn they were going to steal whatever my hidden powers were. It didn't end well for them."

It was silent then and I was no longer in the mood to eat. I felt like crying and I didn't like that about myself. I cried so easily and rambled off trivial things, very poorly, when I got around new people. Pushing my chair back I stood saying, "I am sorry for the rambling, but I am suddenly not hungry anymore. I think I feel rather tired from the flight."

Knox grabbed my hand saying, "Do not let my cousin bully you!" He spoke this loudly before lowering it to a soft whisper, "And you were not rambling. You were merely answering a question. Some people tend to lie; however, you spoke honestly and that says something about your character. You should never be ashamed about being who you are."

Taking a good look at him, I found him to be rather handsome, in a Poseidon sort of way with eyes the color of the sea, to die for lips and a thick hooked shaped nose – which looked as if it was once broken. Even though he was trying to make me feel better, I couldn't help but let a few tears fall, before sitting back down replying, "I'm not letting him bully me. I just really don't feel all that great. I feel a nap would make me feel better." I stopped to look at my bowl before looking back at him, "I think the queasy feeling has more to do with the smell coming from the soup. I'm not too certain, but it smells like fish or something close to it. I don't want to seem rude by not eating it or asking for it to be taken back."

He let go, as Stan's mother said, "If that is all, it is very considerate of you. We should have asked if there was anything you and your friend… Bridget, was it?" I nodded to confirm before she continued, "had any dietary restrictions."

Looking up, I could see everyone else resumed their meal. Everyone that is, but Stan, who stared at me angrily for some reason. Turning my eyes back to Stan's mother, I answered her as she ate, "The only thing that I am allergic to is garlic and pepper. That's any peppers too – bell peppers, lemon pepper, regular pepper, and oddly enough, Dr. Pepper. They make my throat swell up shut. I don't like fish, or anything from the sea for that matter, because it has a foul smell of seaweed, sea scum, and tainted water. It makes me feel very nauseated, but I can eat fried sea foods, fish sticks, and tuna from a can just fine. Not sure why that is, but I do think it's weird."

Half way through my mini speak she turned her eyes to me, chuckling, "That is quite a list. I will make sure the chef knows about your allergens and preferences, however, I do not believe you will be able to eat anything today as the menu has everything on your list....

"Oh, where are our manners? You do not know all our names. I am Corliss Moren and sitting next to me, here, is my husband Eldon Moren. You already know our son, my nephew Knox and his twin sister Kimberley Newell. Across from you is our head of security, Dayton Moren; he is also Athelstan's cousin and my husband's nephew. Sitting next to Dayton is Sherwood Read, along with his parents Raleigh Read and Yedda Preston-Read, and their daughter, Storm." She paused as each person waved a brief howdy-dee-do, before adding," I am sure if you are dead set on going to London, my husband and Dayton can work something out. You may not get to do everything that you want, but that would be better than nothing."

This made me completely happy and I started bouncing in my seat. "Oh! That would be awesome, if it would be alright."

Dayton piped in snapping, "As for London we will have to wait and see. If it is possible for us to make a trip, then we would need to leave here at four o'clock in the morning and be back no later than midnight." Inwardly I groaned, and nodded because – despite his drop-dead fineness, as Bridget would say – his bipolar tendencies scared me.

For most of the meal I sat in silence. Every now and then Knox would ask me random questions. Most of his questions were about America and the politics. He had a hard time grasping the concept of Democracy and the need to vote people into office.

It was towards the end of the meal, Knox started asking questions about me. Where I was from? What I liked to do for fun? If I had any siblings?

My siblings interested him the most, for some reason. "Really, you have six other siblings?"

"Yes, three older and three younger."

"I bet that was fun growing up."

"It had its moments." Knox looked curious and hoped I'd elaborate more on the subject. When it came to my family, and especially my siblings, I tended to clam up, usually saying one word or a brief remark. Bridget was the only one who knew about my family.

When I didn't say more, Knox asked, "What is your profession?"

Confused, I asked, "Profession?"

Frowning, he explained, "Yeah. I already know you are a writer, however, that sounds more like a passion, than a career. When you are not writing, what do you do to pay your bills?"

"Oh, I work at a motel as a housekeeper. I don't want to do it forever, which is why I write, but I would like to purchase my own little inn, someday."

It was then, the last course was brought in and I quickly took a bite of the battered fish. It put an end to whatever he was about to ask next. As I ate the only dish I could, I realized Dayton had been quiet throughout the rest of the meal. Looking up, I saw him staring intensely at me. I didn't think I had anything on my face, but he stared at me, much like the stewards from the plane. It felt very unnerving. *What is it about me that makes these people stare at me, as though I sprouted a third head?*

Stan was the first to excuse himself from the table. Then, the Reads said their goodbyes to the Morens. Mr. Read told Dayton he would get him some documents he'd requested, before completely dismissing himself. Before long, it was just Knox, Dayton, and me left at the table. Finishing the fish, I went to take my leave, but Knox stopped me asking, "Would you like me to help you find your room?"

Blushing, I pulled the map from my corset and said, "No. I should be able to get back with this map." Unfolding the map, I laid it out on the table.

Dayton frowned, asking, "Nicole, can I see that?"

"Umm…, sure." I said, pushing the map towards him.

He let out aloud a rumble that shook the table. It was frightening because his eyes seemed to change completely black for a split second, before returning to normal. Growling, "You will never find your room on this map because it would seem it is a half map. Half the corridors are missing along with some of the rooms. This map is also upside down."

I felt incensed. "So... Stan gave us a false map put in our rooms?" Dayton nodded as Knox took the map from him to get a better look. "Why would he do that?"

"It does not matter why. I will bring you a working map," Dayton said, walking off.

Resigned, I said to Knox, "I guess I should take you up on that offer or I may never find my room again."

"I am happy to help." Knox said, leading the way. He was a sweet, young man, but I got the impression he was hoping for more than friendship. I wasn't sure I was ready for any kind of romantic relationships.

The whole way to my room Knox rested his hand on the small of my back, that was until Dayton showed up. He followed us the last two turns, to the corridor with my room. I paused outside my quarters feeling like I should say something, but I didn't know what.

Dayton made the first move, by handing me two pieces of paper, saying, "Here is an updated map that will help you make your way through the halls. I brought a second spare map for your friend because I figured her map is a fake as well."

Taking the maps, I whispered, "Thank you, both of you for all your help." Then, I went into my room and shut my door quietly, behind me. I was happy they didn't follow me in.

CHAPTER 7

The Mortal Witch

After dinner, I went to my room, as quickly as I could, without being seen by the witch's observant eyes. *The irritating half-witted wench had been practically bragging about her magic at the table. I can tell Dayton is even pissed with her! He hates witches as much as me. Possibly even more so than me and I am the one who is cursed.*

It was not my fault the vile enchantress and her warlock husband had such a weak child. They pathetically arranged for her to marry an immortal because it was the only way to save a body, as frail as hers, from the airborne diseases in the mortal world. The marriage would have worked if I had not found my twin soul and did not loathe mortals so much. The confounded girl killed herself when she caught me in a lovers embrace with my twin soul. I did not even know about her death until it became the talk of the castle. All the servants had been whispering and gossiping about it for days, before I caught wind of it.

When I asked my parents, they were enraged because I apparently had been told the evening it had happened. I must not have been listening and did not care. I was free to marry my beloved. They became more furious when I asked when I could get married to my twin soul. My mother had screamed at me, for an hour, about keeping to the customs and showing some sort of remorse. I played along, but I had no regrets and I did not have any compassion left in my bones to feel sorry for anyone. Well, no one except Dayton, who was in a prearranged marriage to a troll of a Cimmerian.

It was our shared hatred of mortals, that Dayton understood why I would never break my enchantment. My twin soul was a sacrifice to the spell, which added a twist to my curse, "Whoever it is to be your bride, must be first your twin soul and second, a mortal." This little tidbit, on how to break the curse, took forty seers' and nineteen prophets to uncover. The only way to break the spell was for me to be with a mortal, which would never happen, leaving me out of the running for ascension to the Shade throne.

Dayton despised power wielders, more so than myself, because of the enchantress's hex and my skipped ascension. He was the next heir and did not want the responsibilities. He was being groomed to take over and could not stand the training, nor the thought of leaving his station. I had been groomed to take over until my family finally gave up on me. Not that I blamed them for it, but it took them a long while to stop believing I would break the spell. I would never fall for a wretched mortal because the *Fates* were not that cruel to settle me with a woman so defenseless. Especially, when they already sent me my beloved Isadora.

Pacing around in my room, I heard that irritating mortal getting to her room with my cousins. The annoying cretin even liked what I had Christa stock in her wardrobe. She loved them, except for the yellow gowns. All the other girls who had won the infernal contests detested those garments. They even refused to come out of their rooms wearing a gown. It took them three to four days before finally emerging, defeated. Except for a couple who came out in their birthday suits. It was both annoying and exhilarating at the same time. I had taken so much heat for it too; however, I had never cared, until now. This one mortal, she did not care one bit about them being out of date and the wench even defended me. My mortal loving cousin, Knox, had to sympathize with her and tell her to not let my bullying get to her. *I wonder what it would take to get under her skin? Even if it is the last thing I do, I will find a way to annoy that vexing mortal witch.*

I could feel the blood pooling into my eyes as Dayton came into my room, followed by Knox and Kimberley. Dayton, I was fine with. Kimberley was okay on some days, but I was not sure today was one of them. Knox and his mortal sympathizing ideals, not at all. I still could not believe how friendly the worm was towards the little, puny witch.

Knox and Kimberley stepped back when they noticed my eyes, having experienced my wrath before, when in a foul mood. Dayton on the other hand, stepped forward demanding, "Stan, calm down. Kimi go to the kitchen and grab a two-liter of *AB Sola*. We cannot afford to have these winners drained." *Dayton never tells me what to do, unless I have done something to piss him off.*

"More like losers," Kimberley mumbled before saying louder, "Okay, Dayton. Be back in a jiff." Then she was gone.

I do not want the AB Sola! What I want is the overly happy mortal gone, along with her friend! The feeling of them being drained sounded quite nice, along with watching their lifeless bodies being tossed on the pyre. Something about the last bit hurt, causing a fierce pain to erupt from my heart, that spread out to my limbs. The shock of the unknown pain released some of my bloodthirst. *Why do I keep getting these weird bursts of pain whenever I think of harming these mortals? I want them both gone! Then, I can die in peace.*

As some of the red faded, Kimberley came in with the Sola. I roughly took it from her extended hand and ripped the cap off, not bothering to untwist it. I chugged it down for some unknown reason. *It is odd, not draining them in the state I am in. Normally, I would have gone after the closest human body. In this case, it would have been the contest winner and her witchy friend.*

When Dayton sensed my need for human blood fade, he asked, "So, my dear cousin, what has you so pissed off?"

"It is that mortal, Nicole. She is just so…."

"Good at making lemons into lemonade?" Knox supplied.

"Yes, and perky. I do not like it."

"Well, it is kind of refreshing coming from a mortal. Besides, are you not the one who hates the female mortals acting like they are big bad bitches? And let us not forget the female gold diggers. You find them equally as irritating."

"Knox, enough. I am now adding perky female mortals, with a positive outlook, to my list of mortal aggravations. I find perky on any being to be vexing."

"At least you do not have to plan a day trip because your mother promised the mortal a visit into London!" Dayton snapped. "A promise your father had not wanted to grant, but since your mother has him wrapped around her little finger, I must now escort the witch, Knox and Kimberley into London. I do not mind taking the two of you, but that witch is a whole other story. While Goldie is escorting the two of you, I have to go with *Nicole* by myself and do all the things she wants to do," He spit venom at the wench's name.

"Waa, waa, waa! At least you can leave! Unlike me! If I leave, I will die!" Starting to feel thirsty again, I calmly suggested, "I could always dispose of her before you have to take her anywhere." The suggestion both excited me and hurt in an unpleasant way that was becoming maddening.

Dayton said through clenched teeth, "No, Stan it is fine." This was his way of saying *not on my watch* and to apologize for reminding me of my inability to travel.

Knox sighed heavily, "Let us not forget, Athelstan, if you hurt either mortal, your father and mother will have your hide! Your mother may even have it mounted on the wall if you do. Dayton if it is a big deal for you to escort Nicole around alone, I could always go with the two of you. Then you would not be alone with her and you can stand a respectable distance away. Besides Sis, no offense, I would prefer not to go shopping with you. I know how you get while shopping."

Kimberley glared at me, "That is fine! Instead of shopping for myself, I will be wasting this trip on the American twats. Since you, cousin dearest, did not give them proper clothes, you will be making it up to me on my next trip. You will be buying me some very expensive things."

With a smirk, "Sure Kimi, whatever makes you happy because I will not be around."

She smiled, then frowned as her brother sighed, "This is your last chance to break the spell. Why are you not willing to at least attempt to make it work with one of these girls? If not the one who is a possible witch, what about the contest winner? She might be good."

"That Knox, will not happen either. She dyes her hair and you know how I feel about high maintenance girls. Therefore, this whole thing is a bust," I said shrugging and dropping on my bed.

Dayton then came over, grabbed me by my shirt, lifted me up off the bed and closer to his face. He growled out, "You had better make it work with the winner! I refuse to be the next King, Athelstan Kirkley Moren! If anything, you should get to know her before you judge her. She may surprise you. As for the witch, I will keep her engaged and out of your way. If you do not, I will make sure that human witch is everywhere you are. Once she is gone, I will make your short existence afterwards miserable."

Wow! For Dayton to threaten me to make this all work, he must be extremely desperate for me to be with my twin soul. Realization hit him as to what he was doing and slowly let go of me.

For now, I will humor him, until I make up my mind. Smiling, I said, "Sure thing Dayton. I will give it a whirl. Only if you take the witch as your girl."

Walking to the door, Dayton angrily ripped it open and turned, just for a second, to glare at me before leaving, slamming the door closed once more. Kimberley sighed, annoyed, "You really should not push him so hard, you know. He is under a lot of pressure right now. Dayton must drill Goldie to take over as the lead guard in the event he must leave his post, unexpectedly, to deepen his training with your father in royal duties. There are not enough hours in his day to accomplish everything. He is hoping beyond hope, you will find the one to break the curse. I think, at this point, he is desperate to help, in any way he can, to make you King. The least you can do is try. Do not even attempt to back down because with everything Dayton has going on, I am sure he would make your last days in hell a living nightmare."

I really do not care what he has going on, however, I know if I do not make an effort, my mum will tan my hide.

Not waiting for an answer, Knox and Kimberley turned to leave. However, I stopped them, "Well, if you are leaving so soon, why not inform the witch supper is at 4:30 and she should wear different clothes. I did not really like her in that yellow one. It washed her out. It made her look like the walking dead." *Coming from someone who is virtually dead, is quite ironic.*

They left, slamming the door once more. I rolled my eyes before going over to my dresser to change into a more comfortable shirt. The shirt my mother said *You must wear to meet the guests for dinner* may be soft, but it makes my skin itch. Digging through my drawer, I found my favorite black t-shirt with red letters saying, *I'm handsome and I know you want me.* My parents found it insulting whenever I wore it, however, it spoke true words. *I am irresistible.*

Changing shirts, I decided to go to my favorite spot in the library to finish reading the book I had started last night, *Twilight*. Kimberley let me borrow it and I found it insulting to all Cimmerians everywhere. We did not sparkle or twinkle in any way whatsoever. She claimed it was what all mortals were reading these days and had become as popular as some Harry Potter series, which she loved. I refused to read any of them, as they were about a populace I really despised.

Walking into the library, I found the witch sitting in my favorite reading spot which caused me to pause. She sat there writing in a notebook and was already in a different outfit. This one was blood red and made my body ache in a way I had not felt without the full moon's assistance. "Little Stan" did not go around, standing at attention, without the moon's pull.

With the click of the door, her head snapped up and she looked right at me. I had to admit the color suited her better and showed off her nice ample curves, making her look stunning. *No do not think like that, she is your enemy and given the chance she will only cause you more trouble.* I quickly began to stomp over to her as her surprised expression turned into annoyance. Stopping just a few feet from her, I snapped, "What do you think you are doing here?! And how did you change so quickly?"

Annoyance was thick in her voice, as she turned back to what she was writing, "Well, after dinner, I went back to my room and worked myself out of that dress. Not easy, by the way, to do on my own. I was practically naked when Knox and Kimberley came in to tell me I needed to change clothes before 4:30, which she told me is suppertime. I am certain I embarrassed Knox because his face turned beat red. Kimberley helped me put on this dress and complimented me on the choice, as it suited me much better than the last one. Although, I must say she is right about one thing." Looking back up at me, she paused, before a sly smile crossed her face. She continued, "She's right about your taste in colors, as well as clothes. They both suck."

"Why you little…" I started before she lifted an eyebrow.

Interrupting, "Excuse me, but I am only speaking the truth. As for what I am doing here, I noticed on the map there was a library and thought I would check it out. I did and found this…," she motioned with her hand to the library, "as well as a few research books. I've needed them for a story I've been working on for a long while now. Plus, this little window seat is perfect for sitting and writing, or even reading for that matter." As she spoke, her annoyed expression turned into a happy smile.

I huffed and stomped my right foot, feeling much like a teenage girl - which annoyed me more than anything else. I growled, "So then... you and your friend are what? Both struggling writers? How is it you pay your bills? Do you both live with your parents and mooch off them?"

Her smile faded into a frown, as she closed her writing book and grabbed the others she found for her research. Standing, she stormed past me, stomping on my right foot as she left. I wanted, so much at that moment, to drain her, but I did not. Not wanting to share anything of mine with her, I was elated to have my spot back to myself. As childish as that was, I opened my book and I picked up where I left off.

CHAPTER 8

The Jerk

Storming into my temporary room, I tossed my notebook and the research books onto the bed. All I wanted to do was put on some night clothes and sit down to work on my story. Searching for a set of nightclothes in the wardrobe, I couldn't help but think about that egotistical jerk. *First, he had purposely arranged for those out of date clothes to be put in my wardrobe and gave me a bogus map. Then, he was completely rude at dinner and just now, crude in the library. What is his deal... where are some pajamas? They should have something in here, but there isn't anything. A person can only look for something for so long and find nothing before giving up. I bet he wants me to sleep nude!*

Annoyed, I took off the gown, as gently as I could in my state, but ended up ripping it anyway. As I tossed the ruined gown onto the fainting couch, I worked on my corset with a little less aggression. Laying the corset on top of the vanity, I opened the bottom drawer that contained my pajamas, I just so happened to think about bringing. I pulled out the red *Hello Kitty* nightshirt and pink *Eeyore* short shorts. They didn't really match, but it wasn't like anybody else would see me in them.

After putting on my night clothes, I climbed into bed and continued with my writing, occasionally looking through the reference books I found in the library. Often, when I was working on a story, I zoned out the world. Having wrote three chapters, I heard a knock on my door, which startled me from my fantasy realm. I shouted, "Come in," as my heartbeat calmed down.

Hearing the door open, I looked up to see Balin standing there looking rather surprised to find me in my pajamas. Tilting my head to the right, I asked, "Yes?"

Letting out a cough, he said, "Miss, those are not appropriate clothes for supper and everyone is waiting on you to come join them in the dining hall."

Going back to my writing I said, "Well, tell them I said to eat without me because I am not all that hungry."

"Miss, the Duchess has had the cooks prepare something special for you," he said, shocked I would refuse to eat with everyone.

Feeling guilty, I looked up and asked, "Is Stan there?" He looked at me confused, then nodded his head, before I continued, "Then, I will not be coming. I shall eat it in here, if that is alright."

"I shall ask," he said, leaving as I went back to my story.

* * *

We had been waiting over an hour for that ghastly witch to enter the dining hall, in order to start eating. My mother had sent Balin to find her and remind her it was supper time. *How hard is it to find one, insignificant, little witch? Apparently, it is very hard, as they have yet to return.* Finally, hearing the dining room door open, I expected to see the little plump witch, but it was only Balin. I ground my teeth together, "You could not find the mortal, Balin?"

He walked all the way to the table and stood behind my parents. Bowing his head, "Regrettably, Miss Holmes wishes to eat in her room. She is in the middle of working on her story."

My parents turned to look at me with fury in their eyes. *They assume it is my fault. They would be correct of course, but I am not going to tell them that.* Raising an eyebrow, I looked at them innocently. "What are you two glaring at me for? I did not do anything to the foolish mortal."

"Then, why does she not want to come down," my father roared, "but wants to stay in her room to work on some story, Son?"

"How should I know?" I asked, point blank, knowing it was a lie.

Balin coughed, then added, "Miss Holmes looked as though she was in the middle of writing something important. She had a lot of books from the library spread out all over her bed. Some were even stacked on the floor, as well, but those on the floor might be some she brought with her."

"Books..." my mother questioned, looking right at me, "by any chance, Son, did you see her in the library this afternoon?"

I did not really want to answer that question, nor deal with my parents yelling at me again over some doltish witch. I simply stood up and left without a word.

* * *

I was nearly finished with another chapter when my door opened, and Dayton came in with a coffee table, followed by two identical twin maids, who carried multiple trays with lids. They set the trays on the coffee table and then took their place on either side of the now open door. Dayton sat on the floor, by the coffee table and waited. Puzzled, I looked at Dayton waiting for an answer. Any answer really, but he said nothing. I turned my gaze to the two blondes, hoping for an explanation, but they looked more nervous and out of place than anything. The girls both had pert lips, rosy cheeks, and a nice little nose, both of which was pointed directly at the other wall. Their pale skin looked nearly translucent on their slender frames, as they wore black slacks and dark grey, housemaid smocks.

"Would you please join me for supper?" he asked, looking at me, with a rather forced smile.

I stared blankly at him, for a moment, before I got up saying, "Ummm…, sure?" He watched me intensely, as I walked to the table and sat down, right across from him. After I was seated on the ground, the twins came over removing the lids from the trays, revealing a small leafy salad with sunflower seeds, shredded cheese, croutons, and ranch. On my right, rested an odd-looking fork. I picked it up as I began to eat it in silence. Silence wasn't all bad, but when others were in the room, it was rather creepy. Especially, when you got the feeling everyone in the room didn't want to be there and the person you were eating with didn't like you.

After I swallowed my second bite, I said, "You don't have to be here, you know. I am perfectly fine eating on my own."

Surprised, he said, "A pretty girl like you should not eat alone."

Setting down my fork, I looked at him questionably, "I know I am not pretty or beautiful by any standards. Thank you though, for the compliment, but I know you don't really like me for whatever reason. You don't need to force yourself to stay here. I can eat and take care of myself on my own. I have been doing it most of my life."

Yet again, surprise lit up his face. "I like you."

45

"Right and I'm Queen Elizabeth. Besides, your tone and aggression speaks volumes."

"You are pretty observant."

"Perceptive, yes."

"How about we get to know each other a little bit better?"

"Okay, shoot."

"You said you are capable of taking care of yourself, but have you ever wanted someone to look after you?" This was a genuine question for once, with no hint of bitterness.

"Well... yeah, but no one has ever offered before. Not even my older brother."

Frowning, he asked, "You have an older brother."

"Yes, but I don't see him that often. When I do it is because his girlfriend left him, or he needs a place to live, or he needs money," I answered, before picking up my fork and taking another bite.

"If he is your older brother, he should be the one to help you when you need it. Not the other way around," he said rather annoyed towards my brother, without having ever met him.

I laughed, practically spitting out my food, "Sorry. It's just that I have gotten so use to taking care of all my siblings. It doesn't really bother me." I began to wipe up the food splatter.

He glared at the mess, asking, "You have other siblings? Why does he not go to them?"

Pausing, I looked up at him, saying, "Well, they wouldn't be able to help him. See, when I was four, our mother died from cancer, that she had been battling since she was a child. As she was pregnant at the time with my two youngest siblings, the twins, Blake and Blaine, almost died with her. The doctor couldn't give her any of the chemo treatments because it could have had side effects for the babies. Claire was only two when Mom died and doesn't remember her. Then there is Tommy, Penny and Jared. Tommy's the oldest and he's always getting into trouble. He spends his time in jail. He now has a life sentence because he's been caught for the same crime, three times. Penny died in a car crash, that she and father were in, when she was sixteen...."

"Dad never forgave himself for it. Since then, it was up to me to make sure we all got to school, got new clothes, school supplies, and had food in the house. Tommy was in the middle of his senior year of high school and dropped out, to make money to support us. Dad quit working at that time and Jared didn't make things too easy on Tommy or me. Jared got a girl knocked up at fifteen and the girl didn't want to get an abortion, but also didn't want the baby. She left their baby with Jared to raise and he didn't want anything to do with the infant. It was up to me to look after her and name her. I always liked the name Tammy and it fit her."

"How old were you when you had to take care of your brother's daughter? What about your dad in all this?"

"He committed suicide just before she was born. I was almost eleven."

He looked rather sad, then said, "I am sorry. I should not have pried."

I smiled at him, laughing, "Well, it's not something I really tell people because I don't want them to feel bad for me. Stuff in life happens and you can't change it. You have to move on and look for a better future. I know to some, it sounds weird and doesn't make sense, but I think it is the only way to live a truly happy life."

Nodding his head, he asked, "How old were you when your sister died?"

"I was eight," I answered, then took another bite.

He sat, staring at me in silence, while I ate the rest of the salad. I always felt like a pig eating in front of people. I didn't know why, probably a human error thing. After the salad plate was empty, the trays were taken away and replaced with another, that had raw veggies and fruit. "If you do not mind my asking, how did your father…."

As I knew where he was going with his question, I interrupted, "Kill himself?" I didn't understand why I was even telling him all this. It was like I had to tell him whatever question he asked me.

"Yes."

"Well, a year after Penny died, he got drunk and a cop brought him home. Jared was at a party and Tommy was working overtime, covering a co-worker's shift. I was left at home to watch the little ones. I apologized for my father's bad behavior. The policeman then helped me to bring my father in and to his bedroom. He was really nice and stayed with me because his shift had just ended. The cop was a father himself and didn't feel right about leaving me alone, with an intoxicated father, to watch over myself, my siblings and my niece. He wanted someone older and more responsible there before he'd leave….

"After a couple of hours, I got this bad feeling and I didn't follow it through, even though I should have. I remember that it was a half hour before Tommy was due home and something told me to go look in on Dad. Honestly, I don't know why I didn't have the officer go with me but when I went into my dad's room, he wasn't there. I went to look for him in his bathroom, thinking he'd be bent over the toilet, from too much alcohol. Everything after that is fuzzy. I don't remember screaming, just a puddle of deep red liquid surrounding my dad on the floor. It never dawned on me, until we were at the hospital being told he was gone, that it had been blood on the ground. I still blame myself because I should have gone and checked on him sooner, but I was busy mending the boys' clothes….

"Anyway, a few months later those of us that were minors got placed in foster-care and separated. The agent said my eldest brother was ill-fit to take care of five minors. We've since lost track of our younger siblings and I've no clue what became of little Tammy," I confessed, whispering the last part while looking at my plate. I didn't know when I started crying, but Dayton's hand gently wiped away my tears with his napkin.

"I am truly sorry. No child should have to go through that," he said lifting my chin to stare at me. He looked sincere in that moment and the feeling he didn't like me had dissipated. All I felt was empathy. I didn't like being pitied, but it was nice having someone who truly cared about me.

"Thanks, but please don't feel sorry for me. There are people in this world who have gone through worse, who deserve the pity more than I do," I said, wiping away the rest of my tears.

His eyes looked sad, but he smiled, "You are something else. You are most definitely not what I expected."

I looked at him puzzled and asked, "What did you expect?"

"Most of the American girls, who have won the various contests my Aunt and Uncle held, are usually very demanding, snotty, expect more than we are willing to give, or are just plain out…," he paused, trying to find the right word, coming up short.

"A bitch," I filled in bluntly.

"I would have gone with complete twats, but yeah. I do not like to use that kind of language in front of women," he replied, with polite suggestiveness.

Laughing, I said, "Well, I won't tell if you won't." He laughed a wonderful, deep belly laugh. It felt like a sound he didn't make all too often.

The rest of dinner we chatted about anything and everything. It was a lot of him asking questions, with me answering. I did ask a few questions, but not that many. He often answered with "I cannot answer that," which was fine, but odd at the same time.

After a while, long after supper was done, he said, "Well, Miss Holmes, it has been a quite enjoyable meal and you have been equally entertaining. But sadly, I need to get back to my duties. I will tell you that we had plans to go into London tomorrow, but it has been postponed until the day after. You will only get this one day and you should try to figure out where it is you would like to go the most."

Frowning slightly because I hoped to spend a few days there, I sighed, "A day is better than nothing. I can tell you right now, as long as I get to see the statue of Peter Pan and the place where Shakespeare put on all his plays, I can leave England a happy American. Those are the two places I've always wanted to see in person. I've seen them in movies and pictures, but it would be absolutely wonderful to see them in person."

He looked at me in awe and confusion but remained silent. Standing up, he bowed to me before leaving. I had never felt more confused in my entire life. When I heard the door close, I got up and took my place back on the bed, resuming my story from where I left off.

I suddenly got really tired as I reached the last chapter for my book. Deciding to stop and finish in the morning, I closed everything up. Looking down at my phone, I realized it read nearly three in the morning. *No wonder I'm tired.*

I moved all of the books from the bed, to the fainting couch, because I didn't want them to get mixed with my books from home. I moved my books up against the wall, this way in the morning I wouldn't trip over them. Then, I placed my notebook I'd been writing in most of the afternoon and half the night, to the top of the stack on the floor. Crawling into bed and under the covers, I nearly fell asleep, until I realized what Dayton had seen me wearing and my mind started racing and didn't stop for another hour.

CHAPTER 9

The Enchantress is Back

After leaving the dining room, I went to the library for a few. It was not long before my mother found me and started yelling at me, for upsetting our guest. Normally, her yelling would not have bothered me, however, I had no patience today. Actually, my patience had been microscopic and with the new moon, it was non-existent. I closed the book I started and left her, as she continued to wail at me the whole way out. I decided since everyone was done eating supper, I could go and eat in peace. I knew I would feel better with some food and Sola, however, this thought was short lived. My mother quickly caught up to me and asked, "Where do you think you are going?"

"I am going to get something to eat or drink in the dining hall."

"No, you are not!" my mother said authoritatively, "I instructed Balin and the chef, you are to go without food, or a Sola, tonight because you walked out on supper. I know you were avoiding us earlier about Nicole, but you need to be polite to these contest winners. Show some kind of interest in them to break this spell. You need them… *we* need them. Play nice with these mortals, or else, Son!"

Storming off to my room, I could not believe my mother. She knew, this close to the new moon, I would be needing more food and blood than normal. Reaching my hallway, I overheard Dayton asking the wench, what she did for as a profession? She looked as though she did not understand his fascination with her. The wench answered, "Profession? Oh, you mean what I do for a living? I am a hotel housekeeper and I write short stories, along with novels, but I am meticulous about everything I write. Bridget calls it my OCD kicking into overdrive and tells me to get over it. She doesn't understand that writing is a process and it doesn't just happen."

"Are you and Bridget not both writers?" Dayton said.

"Ummm, something like that." The wench answered. *What does that mean?*

"What do you mean?" Dayton asked.

"Well, Bridget is more of a tall tale storyteller, while I am more of a diary keeping storyteller." The mortal replied.

"But..., Bridget wrote the winning story for the contest?" Dayton asked, and Nicole mumbled something I could not quite catch; however, her face took on a red tone and her expression changed to one of guilt when Dayton exclaimed, "Wait, you wrote the winning story!?"

"Yeah, she borrowed one of my short stories and entered it because she knew I wouldn't have. I quit entering writing contests because I never won them. I have actually entered the contest your family has held in the past and never even made it through the preliminaries. I never entered "Whose The Big Bad Bitch" or "The Survivor Challenges." I am a survivor, but only capable of surviving society, not the wilderness. I have been told I am too damn nice for my own good, which is totally true. I like being nice and positive because so few people are." *She should have become a nun, spewing off such things.*

"Your friend stole and cheated. She should be disqualified and sent back." Nicole squirmed, but Dayton was right. The two of them should be sent home. However, the thought of the witch leaving, left a hole in the pit of my intestine, which I abhorred.

"I agree. It wouldn't have mattered, though, because if I had entered and won, I would have brought Bridget with me."

"I see, then your secret is safe with me." *Might be safe with you, but not with me.* Then, he asked, "What kind of things do you write about?"

"Mostly supernatural stuff. For example, I write a lot about werewolves and vampires. I do have a series on mermaids and another one on faeries. But, mostly I write whatever pops into my head. Usually though, if I don't write it down it bothers me until I do, but I try to make most of my supernatural stories something people have never heard before. I use most of my extra money on buying books on those subjects. That way I always know whether it has been written before. I must say, the idea of vampires not being able to go out in the sun or sparkle doesn't sound appealing to me. I don't believe someone should look like they went swimming in a pool of glitter. It's not a great look on a anyone."

Dayton actually laughed at that! It is not funny! Some mortals actually liked the look, especially since they are always writing about it. He would not know that though, as he never reads anything, other than the newspaper. How can he sit there while using the mortal terms for our people and that of the Therianthropy (ther-e-an-throw-pee) Shade? Even the Therianthropies, K-9 and feline counterparts would have ripped her a new one. They find the term werewolf as derogative as Cimmerians find the term vampire.

Annoyance rising, I stormed past and went into my room slamming the door closed. *Dayton hates mortals and especially witches, more than I do. Yet, he is actually having a nice time with that putrid little wench?* Pacing back and forth, across my room for nearly three hours, I heard a knock on the door. I did not know if I wanted to talk or see anybody else today, but if I did not, things could get worse. With a low growl, I snarled, "Come in."

Of course, it would be Dayton. He is the last person I want to see at the moment. Turning on him, I snapped, "How dare you come in here after you got all chummy with that mortal witch? Get out of here before I lose my temper on you!" I knew my eyes were showing red from my anger and thirst.

He sighed, "I was only chummy with her, my dear cousin, so that when you try to make things work with her friend, she will not find it odd how I am always around her, while you are always with her friend. If she believes I like her, then everyone else will including her friend." It did make sense, but I was still ticked, as well as very thirsty.

Dropping down on my bed, I folded my arms over my chest, "Fine... that makes some sense, but she is still the most annoying mortal I have ever met!"

He laughed at that saying, "You say that about every mortal you meet. What, dear cousin, makes her more annoying than the others... other than her being a witch?"

Glaring, I said, "She sat in my spot in the library!"

Horror crossed his face at that because no one, who wanted to live, sits in my spot. The last person who did, lost an arm as well as a full pint of blood. It may have been a bit dramatic but having been stuck in this castle and not able to go out, had made some things sacred. The library window seat was as sacred as they came around here.

"Well, you had to have some self-control, since she did not end up dead, like the last mortal," he said.

"No… she is lucky she was bright enough to move. I may have insulted her, which is why she refused to come to supper," I replied with a smirk.

I saw that twinkle in his eye as he asked, "What did you say that insulted her?"

"I said, 'you and your friend are what… both struggling writers? Then, how is it that you pay your bills? Or do you both live with your parents and mooch off them?' It seemed to do the trick," I answered, grinning from ear to ear. Dayton's smile faded into a frown and looked pissed off. *Ahhh… I thought he didn't care.* Growling, I snapped, "What is it? Are you trying to hide the fact that you secretly like the…?"

"That is not it Athelstan! What you said was a low blow, as Nicole's parents are both dead," he growled back. *Whatever! It is not like I care about her and neither should he! Yet, he does.* Neither one of us spoke, then Dayton left slamming my door, once more. *That is fine with me! I did not need to be yelled at by anyone else today. There is no way he will ever get me to feel guilty over that mortal.*

Throat burning with need, I had two viable blood bags sprawled out for me to dine on, which made my thirst worse. One though, I needed to fall for me, but the other was a nuisance, with no worth. I could go and kill her; however, I could still hear her working on whatever she was writing in her room. *The pain is back again, and I do not care in the least because it is her time to die.*

She finally went to bed after three in the morning. Seeing red as my throat was on fire I thought, *That mortal witch stands no chance of living after tonight.* I knew the only way I was going to get what I wanted was to sneak into her room, as quietly as I could or maybe even quieter. Opening my creaky bedroom door, I stepped out into the hallway and tiptoed over to Nicole's door. My body screamed to turn around and leave her be, however, I did not listen. Slowly opening what blocked my entrance, I stepped in. Hearing her heavy breathing told me she was in a very deep slumber.

Slowly, I crept over to her bed. It was hard to see in her room with all the candles out. A fact mortals got wrong, about the Cimmerian people, was we could see in the dark, but only demons have eyes to pierce through the pitch blackness. Stumbling, I picked up on her heart as it started beating faster in her chest. Not caring, I paid no attention to the unusually fast pace and stared at her blackened shape. Lifting my hand, I carefully brushed her hair off to the side. My hand shaking, I carefully used my fingers to locate the major artery that held my sweet relief. However, I realized her mind was open for once and I could see into her dream. Looking into her mind, I realized the reason for the rapid heartbeat. In her dream, she ran through a forest. A forest, I had not seen in years... for as many years as I had been cursed.

Someone chased after her, but no one appeared to be pursuing her. Tripping, she fell and knew if she did not get up, she would end up dead. I could not help but smile because she was about to die in a dream, as well as real life. Before she could get up, an old, wrinkled hand grabbed her, pulling her into a standing position. The wench thought, resigned, "Not the Old Hag again," as the hand held on tightly to this poor, helpless mortal. I had the urge to wake her, however, did not. Nicole's eyes then fell on the owner of the hand. Seeing her face caused me to let out a low growl because it was the witch who cursed me, Luella Miller.

Nicole then yelled, "Let go of me! I don't know who you are! Why won't you leave me be?" She began to pull herself away from the witch, only the witch's grasp got tighter and the scenery around them changed to that of her friend's room. The little wench did not notice the change until the Old Hag spoke. The new place caused the wench more fear.

"You must leave, little Nicolette, or bad things will happen to you and your friend. Watch..." the Hag said, turning Nicole towards me and her friend. In her dream, I was sinking my teeth into Bridget's skin. Nicole screamed, both in her dream and out loud. Loud enough to drag the attention of several people in the castle. I knew I should flee back to my room because I could hear them running towards the wench's room. Of course, it had to be my father and Dayton who entered.

Dayton dropped his lantern, extinguishing its flames, to grab me around the neck. Pulling me away from Nicole he slammed me into the wall by her bed. Growling, I gasped for breath. However, I was not interested in getting it back as I was more interested in the young witch's mind. My mother and cousin Kimi came running into the room as Nicole exclaimed, "Bridget! No! Who are you and why the hell are you showing me this? What do you want from me?"

In her dream, Nicole could not move because the Old Hag still had her in a vice grip, keeping her from her slowly dying friend. Luella looked straight towards me saying, "You will never be free from my curse! Nicolette, if you and your friend depart from here, then I will leave you be."

Hhhmmm... how does she know I was watching the witch's mind and why does she want these two mortals gone? Could it be that one of them can break me free of this curse? Hope built up inside of me, until I thought of my beloved Isadora. Then, I saw Nicole jerk herself free of the old hag. She squared her shoulders snapping, "Why the hell should I listen to a word you say? How do I know any of this is real? It could be something you cooked up to scare me into believing you, so that we would leave."

The Old Hag, smirked, then sweetly said, "You, my young seer, should know by now what you see will happen. If you refuse to heed my warnings, you are on your own. Do not come crying to me when your friend ends up dead." Turning around, the old woman went to leave then stopped to add, "You have seen enough death in your young life, Nicolette. What would you do to save your best friend, your close sister, from meeting her end?" The Hag vanished with a puff of smoke and Nicole seemed to relax into a more peaceful sleep.

My eyes focused in on Dayton, who still held my neck tightly. He pulled me away from the wall, then slammed me once more into it, growling, "Cousin, what do you think you are doing in here?"

My father sat by Nicole's side, looking her neck over for any marks, while my mom and Kimberley looked at her worriedly. Standing up relieved, my father said, "He did not bite her. However, we definitely heard her scream." Turning his eyes towards me, "Son, what are you doing in Nicole's room?" He looked perplexed by the fact that I had not killed the witch. I had no reason to hate her now because she was not a witch, but a seer. *They should probably know what went on in her dream. I am not sure I want them to know about her being a seer. It did explain why I could not hear her thoughts when she was awake because Seers have a natural way of blocking out my kind while conscious.* It was the sad fate of seers to be seen as evil, to other mortals. It was a miracle she was alive now. Seers often got killed because of their compassionate ways. They either died from mortals trying to exorcise them from possession or Cimmerians were drawn towards the scent of their sweetened blood. A Cimmerian who drinks a seer's blood ended up with their gift of sight. *I always thought seers were more beautiful... and extinct.*

Once again, Dayton slammed me against the wall. Getting pissed off, I gasped, "I was only looking for a late-night snack, since I was forced to go without any supper. Mum made it clear earlier because of my supposed mistreatment of the wench, Nicole, I could have nothing to eat or drink. She even made Balin and the chefs obey her decision. How was I to know the little wench would start screaming in her sleep?"

The look in Dayton's eyes told me he was not convinced. He knew when it came to my meals, I never held back drinking from a live source and draining them dry. Looking at her sleeping form he growled, "What stopped you?" My dear cousin had the gift of knowing the truth.

Before I could speak, my eyes pooled more blood and I became blinded by the dark color. Carrying me by the throat to the kitchen, he threw me into a chair. Dayton understood what my body desperately needed... food, and wanted me away from the mortals. Since the cooks were in bed, Dayton started cooking me something to eat. A century ago, he had taken up cooking lessons with our chef at the time. While I waited for him to finish cooking, he gave me a can of *O' Be Positive Sola*. Dad, Mum, and Kimberley followed us from Nicole's room as they were curious to why I had hesitated to drain the little seer. It was out of character for me to leave a mortal be, when I clearly wanted blood.

Sitting there enjoying the food Dayton made, I said between bites, "I only hesitated because Luella showed up in Nicole's dream, warning her to leave here. It was curiosity that kept me at bay, since the old hag seemed hell bent for them to leave. I think the hag believes one of them can break the curse."

Everyone started talking at once. They all kept asking, "Are you certain? What did she say exactly? Why was Nicole dreaming of her?"

I could not keep up and shouted, "One at a time! Please!"

Dayton then asked, "Is it true... one of them can break your curse?" He sounded a bit too hopeful by the idea of my spell being broken, however, I held no hope in it at all.

With a cheeky grin, I said, "Yes, I believe so. I do not think it is the first warning the old hag has given Nicole."

Father then said, "The warnings started before she even boarded the plane. Nicole must be a powerful witch to be able to get a strong connection with someone dead. Especially, one trying to ward her off from this place, at such a distance. Son, you must try to get close to one of them and since you already have a great disinterest in Nicole, your only option is Bridget. I know how you feel about mortals, however, you must try."

I am not going to say anything because I know the importance of finding my twin soul... but honestly, why a mortal? I do not want to choose either of the mortals, however, Nicole is dangerous, especially, if she is a seer. I would not have wanted to accidently inherit her gift of foresight, as it was common for Cimmerian Shades to gain their gifts from a just a single drop. Most Cimmerians ended up going insane from seeing the future. *I suppose this is what people refer to as a double-edged sword. No matter, I will just go after the weaker mortal and be done with this curse. Once we are married and the curse has ended, I can always kill her instead of changing her. It will be nice to move on from this disaster.*

CHAPTER 10

The Sleeping Beauty Awakens

I woke up groggy, trying to understand why my bed was shaking so much. Then Bridget's voice broke through the fog, whining, "Nickies will you wake up please. I really have to go to the bathroom and I can't find the toilet."

Pulling the heavy blanket over my head, I asked, "What time is it?"

There was a pause, one long enough that I nearly fell back asleep, but then I heard her say, "It's six-twenty-three in the morning. Now, will you please tell me where the toilet is?"

I groaned saying, "Through that door on the right-hand side." I poked my hand out from under the covers to point in the direction of the door I spoke of. Listening to her move quickly to the door and I heard it slam shut. I fell back asleep, only to hear the door open once again.

She whined, with more urgency this time, saying, "I don't see a toilet. There is the same stupid tub, bowl, and pot I found in mine. I don't see any toilets, unless they are invisible or pops out of the wall, it isn't in there. Nickies, I really have to go. Please, come show me the toilet?"

Throwing the covers off in annoyance, I stormed over to the bathroom and entered it heading toward the large pot. Doing a hand motion of a girl from *The Price Is Right*, I showed off the goods of the chamber pot, saying rudely, "This is the toilet. It is called a chamber pot. You can either use it or go find an unoccupied bush outside. I don't care one way or the other. Now, if you don't mind, I was up late last night and am tired. If you must wake me again, you better be dying or already dead." I was a mean morning person, especially when I first woke up and she knew that.

As I walked past her and back through the door, I stopped as Bridget screamed, "A chamber pot?! This place doesn't have indoor plumbing! Are we back in the middle ages?!"

I sighed, "I told you if you don't like it go outside and use a bush, otherwise use the darn pot and be happy. I iz going to's go'z back to sleepy-bye." Closing the door, she started to cuss up a storm, but used the pot anyway.

Climbing back into bed to get cozy and head back into lala land, Christa came in saying, "Oh good, Nicole. You are up. I was sent to see if your friend had awakened yet, however, she is not in her room. I thought, maybe, you might know where she is? I was also told to wake you up as well. I am to help get the both of you dressed and ready for the morning," she giggled, while I groaned inwardly, before she continued. "That, and to make sure you and your friend wear something you like and are comfortable. I am to make sure you two are ready and down for breakfast, which is in about an hour. If I am to succeed, we must get started or the two of you will never be ready."

I groaned out loud and snapped, "Fine, but I don't do early mornings! Bridget is in the bathroom using the pot and not too happy about it. She won't be happy having to wear the clothing in her wardrobe, just to forewarn you. She, however, knows better than to fight with me this early in the morning. I can help, if she gives you hell for it."

Climbing out of bed, I began to remake it out of habit. I was certain that I wouldn't be able to go back to sleep any time soon. After I finished straightening out the bedding, Bridget waltzed in, emerging from the bathroom. Noticing Christa, she stopped, asking, "I thought you were going back to bed and who is that?"

"This is Christa. She's our chambermaid and she is here to get us dressed and ready for breakfast, which is in an hour. I swear, Bridget, if you don't do as she says, or you fight over what you must wear… I promise you I will blow a gasket all over your make-up kits and flush them down a toilet when we get back home," I told her crossing my arms.

"You wouldn't dare," she said aghast.

"Try me," I glared at her.

"Fine," she snapped.

I started to head towards Bridget's room, but Christa grabbed my arm saying, "Nicole, shall we get you dressed first, since we are already in your room?"

I looked at her as though she must have been insane. I knew it wasn't her fault as she didn't know me all that well. Nor, did she know that Bridget took forever to get ready for anything. Rolling my eyes, I said, "Bridget will take way longer to get dressed then I will. We'll start in her room, get her dressed and help her put her face on afterwards. I am not all that picky and will take about ten minutes to get ready."

Leaving my room, I walked to Bridget's new dwellings both drowsy and irked, with the two of them in tow. Naturally, Bridget didn't have anything unpacked. I knew if Christa didn't start getting Bridget ready, we would never be on time. I also knew her bags needed to be emptied, of all her paraphernalia, if we were ever going to have time to get me ready. Bridget was always lazy about things, and if she had her way, she would live out of her luggage the whole stay. Looking at Bridget, who looked sheepishly at the wall, I sighed, "Christa, you'll need to work on her, while I unpack her bags, or it will take longer if I don't. Bridge is absolutely lazy about unpacking and if she has her way she'll remain packed throughout our stay."

Christa nodded and pulled Bridget over to the wardrobe. The moment the wardrobe opened, and Bridget saw what she was to wear, she yelled, "I am not wearing those medieval torture devices!"

I snapped at her, "Cut it out or I will flush your good perfumes down our toilet, Bridge!" Pouting, she settled down. While they went through the gowns, Bridget complained about each one. I picked up her bags and neatly stacked them before I began to empty out each one. It took longer to unpack because Bridget packed as though she would never be coming back. It was insane to pack that much, but Bridget thought it was normal.

The nice thing about our rooms was that they had the exact same layout – even the color scheme was the same. It made it easier to organize her many belongings. By the time I finished, the only thing Bridget had left to do was her makeup. Bridget didn't look too happy in her gown and snapped at Christa, "I can put on my own makeup! I don't need any help from anybody else, anymore. Now, Shoo!"

Bridget had always been very beautiful in that old-fashioned kind of way. The light brown dress she had on only made her skin look all the more brilliant. Looking at the pink flower design, the ugly, green monster began to rear its ugly head. I hated this the most about myself. She was the only person who had ever brought that part out in me and she was my best friend. It may not have been so bad, seeming so beautiful inside and out, even though she cheated on all of her boyfriends. Every guy dreamt of being the lucky one to catch her eye and it was never like that for me. Although, most of those guys she went out with, only wanted one thing... sex. That was something I would never give any guy because I was sadly, still a virgin. I didn't believe that two people should do such an act, for the simple fact that they could. All I had ever wanted was to give myself to someone I loved and who truly loved me in return. For me, I wanted him to know that I waited just for him. To give him something no one else had.

I sighed and left, going back to my room. Christa followed me, and we went straight to the wardrobe. Running her hand over the gowns, she asked, "You are not a morning person, I take it? Or, do you act crabby when you first wake up?"

Taking a seat on the fainting couch, "The only reason I should be up right now is if I had to go to work or school, and/or someone close to me has died. So, to answer that... no! I am not a morning person and Bridget knows better than to wake me up this darn early," I yawned before asking, "Will there be any coffee or maybe a whole pot of caffeine? That is about the only thing that will get me through this day."

As she didn't answer, I took it as *no. Great! I am going to be one crabby girl, all day.* As I sat, Christa went through all the dresses and took out a very beautiful, dark red dress with golden vines woven intricately into the fabric. As she showed me the gown, my excitement started to bubble up for the first time this morning. The sleeves flared at the wrists and I couldn't wait to put it on. Standing up, I took the dress from her and laid it where I had been sitting. I knew by the look of the fabric my corset wouldn't work because the lace on it would show through. Bending down to the bottom of the wardrobe, I grabbed out the whale bone corset. It was not my favorite choice, but it was the only corset that would make the gown look proper.

Christa tilted her head to the side asking, "I thought you preferred your own corset over the whale bone one we provided."

"Well, yeah... but my corset has lace and from the look of the dress, it would show through and look odd. The whale bone, though, won't and I can always change after breakfast," I said. Then, I tried once more to ask, "Will there be coffee?"

Christa looked rather timid as she answered, "No coffee... but there is caffeine in the tea we have. Ummm, I am not sure if there will be a pot of it, though."

With a sigh, I resigned, "That is fine. So long as it has caffeine in it, I can make do." She smiled, and we got to work on getting me dressed.

Once I had the breath-taking corset and the gown on, Christa had me sit down on the vanity stool where she started to French braid my hair. I wasn't sure what she used to tie it off as it was invisible. Turning to the mirror on the vanity, I stared at my amazing reflection. The way she French braided my hair looked like a crown, starting on either side of my part, going up to the center of my head and back into one braid. Due to the blonde highlights, it looked as though I had gold strings woven into it. Those strings made my ordinary brown hair look brighter, shinier, and even healthier. I have never seen myself look magnificent, nor radiant.

It took Christa a while to awake me from my shock because I was entranced by my appearance. I didn't hear her, nor Bridget, call my name. Once the awe wore off, I was vaguely aware of Bridget saying, "Nicki... Nicki did you hear Christa? We have to go to the dining hall."

Snapping out of my stupor, I turned to hear a gasp from Bridget and saw a pleased smile on Christa's face. Turning back around to look in the mirror, I frowned saying, "Yeah, I heard you that time, but is there something wrong with my face?"

Bridget laughed, saying, "Nothing is wrong... you look *so hot*!" I spun back to look at her because she was always telling me that I needed to look hotter. Sometimes even saying I needed to be sexy, but she has never once told me I looked hot.

Confused, I asked, "Do I look that good?"

Christa nodded while Bridget said, "Even though these aren't todays fashion, I must say the medieval look is totally your scene. I would bet that you get a few sizzling looks while wearing that."

"Thanx Bridge, you are looking pretty hot yourself. I doubt anybody will be looking at me with you around. Besides, I think we should head down for breakfast, before we are late."

Before she could rebuff my comment, her stomach growled, making her realize how hungry she really was. Turning slightly to the side, she gestured for me to lead the way. I did just that, as I lifted up the front part of my dress a few centimeters to avoid tripping. Christa handed me the new map as I passed her on the way out, Bridget right behind me. I could hear Bridget the whole way down to breakfast trying to figure out how to walk in her gown. It did not take me as long today to get to the dining hall, as yesterday, with the full version of the map. The doors opened on their own, once again, to reveal the group of people I met the other day. I smiled as I saw an empty chair sitting right next to Dayton.

Walking toward our seats, all the men stood, while my eyes never once left Dayton's. I had never met anyone with such an air of mystery before. A mystery that screamed at me to be uncovered, which was quite odd because I had always been good at reading people and instinctively sensing all their secrets. However, with him, it was as though he kept such a tight lid on everything, much like I did. Strangely, he was the first person I had ever talked to about my past, after just meeting one another. I did not even tell Bridget about it, for three years, and she was my best friend. With Dayton, it was as though I felt compelled to tell him anything and everything he asked of me.

Bridget sat down before me and Dayton held out the chair next to him for me to take. After I sat, all the men resumed their seats, with the exception of Stan, who once again remained seated and whose gaze was on Bridget with morbid curiosity. *He is an enigma that I cannot understand and really do not want to.*

The moment everyone was seated once more, Knox grinned at me and said, "Nicole, you are looking ravishing this morning."

Blushing, "Thank you, Knox."

After that, everyone at the table didn't waste any time asking Bridget questions with the exception of Dayton. The more I watched and listened to everyone, the more I became invisible. When around Bridget, it always seemed to happen. Sometimes, so much, that it felt as if I might have disappeared altogether. One thing that did make me giggle was how everyone kept referring to Bridget as Sleeping Beauty.

Dayton then brought me back from the inferno, asking me, "How long have you known, Bridget?"

"Well, I have known her since half-way through our tenth-grade year of high school. So... about eight years," I told him. There was something in his voice that sounded different from last night. It almost held an edge of anger and some regret. It was unsettling, to say the least, but I thought it better to ignore it.

"How did you meet?" He then asked.

"Ummm, well… we met in fifth period P.E. We were assigned to be partners and she didn't quite want me for a partner. I was really awful in the athletic department. I was always hurting myself or others and because of that, no one wanted to be partnered with me. The teacher had to do rounds with all the students in the class to keep it fair. Anyway, that day we were partnered, she got hurt badly, but thankfully it was just a very bad sprain. However, the way she carried on, you would have thought that she had broken something. Needless to say, because of that sprain, the guy she was crushing on dearly, finally asked her out. Then, for whatever reason she started sitting with me and talking to me more and more. At first, I thought she was using me to get guys, but then I soon realized that we were best friends and have been ever since," I replied. After I answered him, he didn't say another word. I was too afraid to ask him any questions because he seemed to be in a very foul mood.

CHAPTER 11

The Morning with Sleeping Beauty

When Bridget and the wench entered the dining hall my father, Dayton, Knox, Sherwood and his father Raleigh all stood up for them. I did not think there was a point to it anymore as it was no longer customary. Once they were both seated, my mother and Yedda started to ask the wench's friend questions. For the most part, I ignored them until Storm asked Bridget if she had any boyfriends.

The powerless wench laughed saying, "I am between boyfriends at the moment, but I am always looking out for mister right." At that, she winked at me, and all I wanted to do was puke. I could tell she was nothing more than a faker.

Everyone laughed mostly to be polite; however, the seer rolled her eyes and my cousin Dayton remained silent. Then, my mother asked, "What made you decide to enter the writing contest?"

This took her by surprise, as I saw wheels in her mind running over different lies for stealing the seer's story. Once she decided on the lie, she said, "Oh, I figured I would win with the story I entered and the free trip with my best friend sounded like fun. She hardly ever gets out. Nicki is always inside working or writing and never finds time to enjoy life." *What a little liar? I cannot believe how fake she truly is.*

My eye focused in on Nicole because *why would anyone want to stay inside? If I had the freedom to leave the castle, I would in a heartbeat!* My eyes moved back to Bridget, as I listened into her lying mortal mind. *I knew more about her than anyone here. Probably, more than her own friend. No one else at this table would think to listen in on her mind because they consider it to be rude, whereas I find it entertaining. It is the only way to find out the true personality of any mortal. This particular mortal had five boyfriends back home, who knew nothing about her or what she wanted. I do not think she even knew what she wanted from a partner.*

This girl liked her friend and liked to take advantage of her because of her good nature. What was more, she seriously wanted to get her friend laid. She disproved of the seer's beliefs on being a virgin, which I found to be a rare trait these days. Bridget felt her friend needed to get out of the bubble she had put herself in. *I happen to agree with this, but I am a sex addict – more so around the full moon – and find the seer's virginity intriguing. However, if not for the fact she is a seer, it would have been a fun chase. Her gift is one I do not want, nor would I want... to tie myself that completely, to a mortal.* Then Yedda asked, "What do you do for a living?"

Laughing she answered, "Currently, I am a beautician, but am secretly working on my law degree. I hope to become a high-end lawyer and one day a Supreme Judge."

"Does that take a lot of schooling? American colleges cost a pretty penny. How do you pay for it?" Yedda asked once more.

"Well, I have a part time job as a beautician and I take classes at night, as well as online courses. My parents were rather smart, as were my grandparents and they both set me up with savings bonds from birth to the time I turned twenty-one. They also set money aside for my college fund. I had nearly half a million from them alone. I have also won four Scholarships for school. Therefore, it is more than covered and I am more than well off," she answered. *Finally! An honest answer, for once.*

"Sounds like your parents had a plan for you in mind and gave you every opportunity possible. My question then is, why are you secretly taking classes to become a lawyer? Would you not want people you care for to know?" My father asked inquisitively.

She laughed getting this odd twinkle in her eyes, "Oh, my parents and grandparents want me to be a lawyer since they are all lawyers. I just don't like to give in to what they want me to do and try to do the opposite as much as possible. It drives them crazy knowing I used the saved money to go to beauty school. I want to make a name for myself that they are not connected with."

"Then, how did you and Nicole become friends? The pairing seems a little odd since Nicole has not accomplished much in her life," my father said, causing Dayton to glare up at him. I knew Dayton had gotten the

411 from the wench yesterday and told my father some of what she had told him. Though Dayton seemed to be very wary on giving all he had learned. I was beginning to think he was actually falling in love with the little seer. *Well, good luck to him on that one.*

Surprised, she said, "Oh, well, Nicole and I have been friends since high school and even though she hasn't achieved much in life, she makes due with what she does have. The manufactured home we live in is hers, which she bought with her own money. I live with her because all I have to do is help pay bills and she pays the space rent and the house payments."

"House payments," Knox asked?

"Ummm... yeah. She owns the manufactured home, but before she did, she had rented out the other two rooms to pay it off more quickly. Once it was paid off, she set money aside and bought a foreclosed, farm style home, with six bedrooms, a barn and forty acres. She rented out all six rooms for a low rate to other college students, then rented out stalls in her barn, and a couple of fenced-in fields, which covered the house payment. There is extra added in, with enough left over to set aside. After a while, she used the leftover money for a down payment for another foreclosed apartment building. She rented out the five apartments, at a rate lower than average, to low income families. She may just be a hotel housekeeper, but she is still very business savvy and a stick in the mud," she answered with a laugh. The seer was rather smart even if she was a pauper. It still did not change her status in my perspective.

Having had enough of the utter nonsense going on at the table, I excused myself to get ready for a walk in the garden, with the lying, little tart. As I left, my father spoke in my head reminding me to play nice and behave myself. *That will never happen. I seriously despise mortals and I loathe these two with a passion. I do not see what the damn witch is so afraid of. It is not like I am going to find true love with either of them.*

Reaching my room all too soon, I changed into a pair of black jeans and my navy, cashmere, V-neck sweater my mother had Kimi buy me from Burberry. It was not to my taste, but I was still the Prince, until my untimely death, and must be dressed accordingly. I pulled on my black, belted, Burberry ankle boots and headed to my spot to read some more from my book, until the time came to *play nice* with the mortals.

After an hour in the library, I met up with Dayton, the wench, and the lying tart in the garden. The garden was not my favorite place in the castle, but girls seemed to like it quite a bit. I did not see the hype. It had a gravel path that led into a maze of various rose bushes, shrubs, and a few trees. Not long after we entered the tart said, "This is a *very* beautiful garden. Made more magnificent with you in it." I started hearing her think of all the things she would like to do to me, if we were alone. The things she had in mind I had never seen before, however, they looked rather enjoyable. Although they spiked my interests, I did not want to perform them with her. For some unknown reason, I changed those images from Bridget to Nicole, in my mind. This angered me to the point that if the tart did not stop thinking her naughty thoughts, I would kill her right here and now, which would not sit well with Dayton.

Trying to distract her and myself, I asked, "What do you think of my castle so far?"

She heaved a heavy, annoyed, sigh, "What I have seen thus far looks rather nice. The garden is pretty, but flowers really aren't my thing." *Those were honest words.* Strangely, I felt the same about the garden because I had spent centuries wandering around the perimeter. There had not been many modifications made to anything within the castle grounds. Then, she asked, "What do you make of your cousin Dayton and Nicole?"

Surprised by her question, I turned my head to look at the two of them. Dayton wore his black slacks and black t-shirt with Kevlar. The seer was still wearing the dark red and golden gown she wore for breakfast. I would have thought she would have changed gowns as the tart had, but she did not. Despite knowing the fact, he was only pretending to like her, Dayton seemed to be enjoying her company. I did not like it at all. I could not tell why, but I wanted to kill my cousin and take his place. *This is not right. I should not want anything to do with her and I should not want to cause my cousin bodily harm. The seer really needs to go.* Turning back around I said, "They look nice together. What do you think?"

Laughing, "Well, it doesn't matter what my opinion is because it is what she thinks that matters. Personally, I believe she likes him."

That statement angered me even more, but calmly I asked, "What do you mean? Why do you think that?"

"Easy! I know my friend and she only smiles like that when she is around someone she likes. Her smile always seems to reach her eyes when she likes someone and that doesn't happen very often. The last time she smiled like that was when she got close to her ex-boyfriend, Timothy," she answered.

This confused me, causing me to stop. "Why was he the last?"

Pausing, she turned sighing, "Well, he was the guy she got engaged to. Nicole broke it off when she found him in bed with *his* best friend."

Nodding I said, "I see. She caught him with another girl."

This she laughed at, as we started walking once again, "No, I wish. Turns out he was gay and I guess you could say it broke her confidence. She has never been the same since." Hearing this gave me flashbacks to a time when I was free to roam the earth. However, the memories came and went like a flash because her situation had been different than my past. Seeing her fiancé in bed with a guy had to be more heart breaking then finding him in bed with a girl. At that moment, the tart started fantasizing about us in bed again. Then, her daydream switched to her other boyfriends back home. *She is truly a freak and I refuse to bed her for many reasons. If I take a woman to my mattress then they would be mine, at least until I was done with them.*

"I see," was the only thing I could say. We continued to walk and chat, though it was mostly her yapping about herself. If I asked about the seer, she would prattle off about random rubbish.

After a while, Dayton and the seer became separated from us. I cared not one way or another – at least that was what I told myself. However, this left me alone with the lying tart. As we walked I got progressively annoyed with the little tart blabbering about poppycock. My thirst started to grow unbearable the longer we walked together.

* * *

Dayton, Stan, Bridget, and I went for a walk in the garden. The garden was beautiful, but as I walked with Dayton it felt like he didn't want to be here. We talked a lot about different stuff, some of it on politics. Usually, I didn't like to discuss politics with anyone because it only led to a fight, but it was quite a pleasant topic with him. We'd stop quite often and at some point lost track of Bridget and Stan. Stan was no skin off my nose, but Bridget was another story. I think mostly due to my dreams of Stan killing her, I didn't quite trust them alone.

After an hour of walking with Dayton, a girl with dark blonde hair pulled back in a military kind of bun, told him that there was a problem needing his attention. She stood five feet tall with a slender build. The kind of delicate frame that said *I may be small and a girl, but I will kick your butt.* Her eyes were the brightest blue-green I had ever seen. Overall, she was gorgeous.

He asked, "Goldie, is it something you can handle?" She shook her head. Dayton groaned, before apologizing to me, as they left me by myself in the garden maze.

I stayed in the garden and smelled the flowers. Sometime later, I found a stone bench and decided to sit. The bench, unlike the rest of the castle, looked newer; it was most definitely from this century. It sat off to the side and faced toward an inner circle. In the center, stood a statue that looked rather old, but well-kept. There was a plaque at its base. Not wanting to move, I figured I would read it before I left the garden.

Sitting on the bench, I enjoyed the warmth of the sun as it came in and out of the clouds. I knew that once the dark grey clouds on the horizon came a little closer, it would be time to head in, as they promised a downpour. But, at the moment the small breeze and the vitamin D was nice.

Suddenly, I heard a murderous wail. Standing up I looked around at the three paths trying to figure out which one it came from. I took the path on my right, running as fast as I could. All I could think was *Please, let Bridge be alive.*

It wasn't easy running in the gown, but I managed until someone grabbed my arm. This made me scream at the top of my lungs. Turning around, I saw a frail girl who looked out of time, as if she did not belong. The dress she wore looked much like mine, only black with grey woven flowers. Her eyes were white, and she had blood pouring from her neck and limbs, causing me to scream once more. It ran down, pooling at her feet. Her face held a pale complexion and very thin lips. Her cheek bones and button nose were extremely defined due to the especially thin state of her body.

If she didn't look dead and intimidating, then she would have been pretty. I tried to pull away from her as she said in a British accent, "You must not leave the grounds. Death awaits you."

I wanted her to let go and leave me alone. In a small voice, I pleaded, "Please! Let me go and go away! I need to find my friend before something bad happens to her. I am sorry for whatever happened to you, but please don't take it out on me!"

"You are the one to undo. *You* are twice born and have perished once. She fears you and will try anything to end your existence. *Death will come if you leave*," she said holding tightly onto my arm. She really started to scare me, and I began to pull harder. After a few hard tugs, I pulled myself free and took off as fast as I could in the heavy gown. I started crying because I didn't want this to be starting up again. I had worked so hard to keep the restless spirits away from me. I didn't understand why I was unable to keep them at bay, now. Too freaked out by the ghost to look back, I kept running not wanting to get slowed down by the restless phantom. Nearing the entrance to the garden, I ended up running right into Knox.

"Woah there, Nicole," Knox said, grabbing my shoulders to prevent me from falling backwards. Worry crossed his face once he saw my tears. He asked, "What is wrong? What happened? Did Athelstan do something bad or say something mean?"

Shaking my head, I tried to talk, but it only came out as short, gasping breaths all staggered and blubbery, "Girl…dead…danger…blood…."

It registered something in him though, and Knox worriedly asked, "Where is she?"

I couldn't tell him I could see the dead, nor where she went. I didn't know where she was and didn't want to open my eyes to find out. Grabbing onto him I cried, "Please! Don't leave me alone."

He pulled me into him, wrapped his arms around me, and petted my hair saying, "Alright, I will not leave you. I will call Dayton and have him come look for your friend."

I didn't understand why he worried about Bridget, but I also didn't know what to say either. While I held onto him in a death grip, soaking his shirt, he called Dayton, who didn't sound too pleased. Just as he shut the phone, Dayton showed up. Dayton pulled me away from Knox, glaring and growling, "Where did it happen?"

His grip was tight, and his voice was mean. It frightened me, and I tried pulling myself out of his grip. Seeing my fear, he let go and I stepped back into Knox's body. Knox wrapped his arms around me and I found comfort in them. In that moment, Bridget and Stan came out of the garden maze. Bridget took one look at me and ran over. She pulled me out of Knox's embrace and quickly engulfed me herself, asking, "Nickies what's wrong? What happened?"

Pointing to the garden I sobbed, "Girl…dead…danger… blood…"

She knew then what had happened and began to stroke my hair in a soothing manner saying, "It's alright Nickies. It wasn't real. You have to remember that. It wasn't real… ok?"

"But… but…but she…she gr-grabbed m-me," I quivered. I always hated it when the dead grabbed me and Bridget knew this more than anything. She then started shushing me and continued to stroke my hair.

Then, Stan's father, Eldon, came yelling, "What the hell has my idiot…?" He stopped short as he saw his son. I couldn't quite tell through my tears, but his voice sounded confused as he said, "Alright, what is going on?"

All the guys said, "No idea."

Bridget said, "Nicki got spooked by a small rodent in the garden. I don't think she will be able to walk on her own. Someone will need to carry her to her room and lay her down in bed for a few. Who is going to do that, because I can't?"

Knox made the first move towards us and picked me up bridal style. Instinctively, I wrapped my arms around his neck sobbing, "Sorry about your shirt."

He started walking saying, "Nicole, it is alright." He walked me all the way up to my room and no sooner had he laid me down gently, I was out. Seeing dead people always exhausted me.

* * *

The tart and I were headed back towards the castle when we both heard the wench scream. Bridget took off scared and worried over her friend. I honestly did not see the point in worrying over a scream. It was not I who caused it, therefore there was no immediate threat. However, when we heard a second scream, I quickly caught up to her as she started running faster. I had to admit, even in that heavy dress and the high heeled shoes, she was a pretty fast runner.

Once we reached the entrance to the garden, we saw my cousins and a blubbering Nicole. Confusion entered Dayton's face as he looked up at me. The tart took off towards her friend. Pulling the wench from Knox, she instantly embraced her, asking, "Nickies what's wrong? What happened?"

The wench pointed a shaky finger towards the garden stuttering, "Girl…dead…danger… blood…"

The tart knew something the rest of us did not and began stroking Nicole's hair in a soothing manner saying, "It's alright Nickies. It wasn't real. You have to remember that. It wasn't real… ok." *What the hell was not real? What the hell is wrong with her? Are they both deranged?* Listening in, I found out that not only could the seer see the future, but the dead as well. She had to be stronger than we thought.

"But… but…but she…she gr-grabbed m-me," Nicole quivered. Lifting an eyebrow, I frowned. Who is *she*? I know none of the female workers here would touch either of them as they would not want the wrath of my father.

At that moment, my father came out yelling, "What the hell has my idiot…?" He stopped as he saw me. He looked as confused as we all felt, when he saw that both girls were fine and safe, with the exception of the blubbering Nicole. Then he commanded, "Alright, what is going on?"

All three of us said, "No idea."

The tart then said, "Nicki got spooked by a small rodent in the garden. I don't think she will be able to walk on her own. Someone will need to carry her to her room and lay her down in bed for a few. Who is going to do that, because I can't?

Knox was the first to move towards Nicole and Bridget. Picking the wench up, she wrapped her arms around his neck sobbing, "Sorry about your shirt." Seeing her in Knox's arms caused the rage to build up inside of me which was ridiculous.

When he said, "Nicole, it is alright," I nearly growled. Dayton, my father, the tart, and I followed them up to her room. The tart accompanied Knox, however, the rest of us stayed out in the hallway. After the wench was in her bed, she passed out, and Knox retreated to the hallway with us. After a while the tart joined us, too.

Folding my arms, I snapped, "Alright, what the hell was that all about?"

The lying tart stared at me blankly, before snubbing me, "I have no idea what you are talking about."

Growling, I moved to throw her into the wall, but my father grabbed me. Growling at her himself, "A human being does not go and scream like that, for no good reason, then cries. I would like an answer and I would like an answer, NOW!"

Folding her arms glaring, before sighing, "Do you believe that when some people die unexpectedly, their soul sometimes gets trapped in our plane?"

We all shared an odd look before my father answered, "Yes."

"Well, that's what happened. Nicki has a gift in seeing the deceased and when they have a strong enough energy left, they can present themselves. She has always struggled with her gift. Normally, it is very gruesome and only very rarely, do they look like us now. Nicki's learned how to block them, but sometimes they break through her defenses. Some are violent and end up hurting her. It's been a while since the last one and it had nearly killed her," she explained. At that Dayton left and went into Nicki's room. Lord only knows why, however, my father, Knox, and myself where shocked into silence. The tart then walked right by us into her room. She paused at the door saying, "Don't let her know I told you. She might freak out on me. I don't know why, but she has it in her head that the gift is from the devil and that others won't understand." Then she closed her door leaving the rest of us in silence wanting to know more.

My father turned toward me before walking away, saying, "Son, I hope you know what you have gotten yourself into." *Ok, what the bloody hell does that mean? I did not get myself into anything! None of this is my fault!*

Knox peeked into the seer's room with a pained look on his face asking, "I wonder who she saw, or what they looked like to her?" He looked back to me and I shrugged because I did not care who she saw. She was just some doltish mortal, who was clearly very gifted, and someone I truly wished to stay away from. I pushed myself off the wall and proceeded to my room.

CHAPTER 12

The London Trip

The next morning, I woke up to see Dayton's sleeping form lying next to me. Startled, I ended up falling off the bed and onto the floor. Landing on my butt, I groaned. He was immediately in front of me and offered his hand. Embarrassed, I said, "Thank You."

He began to turn me around to check that I was alright. Finding no bruises, he asked, "Are you ok?"

"Yes, I was just startled to see you in my bed, is all."

Shaking his head, "I am sorry for scaring you, however, I wanted to know that you were alright after what happened yesterday."

"Yes," I answered laughing, "I am feeling much better now, thank you for asking."

He looked worried and asked, "What happened after I left you?"

I didn't want to tell him that I saw a bloody, dead, wandering soul because I didn't know how he would react to it. Most people didn't understand. I had a foster family beat me nearly to death and then had me "exorcised" of the devil. Telling people, besides those I trusted, wasn't something I could take a risk on. I didn't really like to lie, but that was what I did, "I just got spooked by a small rodent, like Bridget said. My imagination tends to run wild when I end up alone."

He didn't seem to believe me, but nodded his head figuring I would tell him when I was ready. I looked down at the floor, feeling rather guilty, when I noticed I no longer wore the beautiful gown from yesterday but a pair of my pajamas. Looking up at him, I asked, "Ummm... who changed me?"

He smiled and backed up saying, "Not me, I swear! Christa and Lady Corliss did. They said you would sleep more comfortably that way. Before you ask, I stood in the hall with your door closed while they changed your clothes."

I sighed, "Oh, ok! That's a relief."

He smirked and lifted his hand up to twirl my hair teasingly, asking, "What would you have done if I had told you I was the one to change you?"

Startled, I looked down as my face heated up saying, "I would have been very embarrassed. I have never been that exposed in front of a guy before."

He lifted my chin then and brought his lips towards mine as he whispered, "I take it then that you are a virgin." I gulped, nodding my head, before he pulled me to him saying, "That is a rare thing in today's society. You best hope my cousin, Athelstan, never finds out because he has a way of enchanting a girl to give up their flower."

Gulping, I stared at his baby blues, whispering, "Thank you for the advice. I don't think I would give him that satisfaction. I firmly believe two people should only partake in such pleasantries by being in love or married first. You could say that I am waiting on my soul mate before I give that one up."

His eyes darkened before he brought his lips to mine with a hunger and need I had never felt from anybody ever. Holding me tightly to him, I felt something grow in my abdomen and it had my stomach tightening in knots. *Oh boy, if I was a normal girl I would so let him take me, but I am not normal, and he knows more about me than I do him. But by gawd, he can kiss like a God.* Removing my lips from his, he growled not wanting me to stop, however, I knew if I didn't we'd do something I totally regret.

He then placed his forehead to mine, growling, "It is probably for the best." Letting me go, he stepped back looking at the door and glared, "You will need to get ready to head out to London. We will be leaving within the hour." I nodded my head because I didn't know if I could rightfully talk, without asking him to kiss me again. Pointing towards the fainting couch he said, "Kimberley brought some clothes she thought might fit you and laid them there."

After he walked out, I slowly made my way to the clothes trying hard to calm myself down. *That kiss was really something.* I had never felt the need to be kissed by someone again as I did now, nor had I ever felt a kiss linger afterwards. This was something new and I was not sure how to handle it. Biting on my lower lip, I thought, *Maybe I could leave it and think on it later or I could sort these feelings out now. I am feeling so many different things, but I really should dwell on it later. Yes, I should get dressed or I won't be going to London.*

Forcing myself to focus on the clothes, I was concerned about whether they would fit. I headed to the vanity and pulled out one of my white support bras and grabbed out a pair of light green bikini underwear. Going back to the couch, I stripped and pulled the bra and underwear on before I pulled on the skirt. The two layered skirt was a pale pink and came just below my knees. It was a little tight on my waist, but it still zipped up. *I am glad I don't feel as though I will pop the seams.* It felt airy and had me wondering if I should put on my skin colored, ice skating leggings. *I probably should wear them, that way I know I'll stay warm.*

Going back to the vanity, I retrieved the leggings, quickly pulled them on and went back to the couch putting on the odd-looking shirt. It was white and on a much slimmer person would have been a bit puffy, but on me it fit more on the snug side. The silk shirt snapped up and a knot made out of the front shirt tails landed perfectly above the skirt. After getting the clothes on, I found a pair of dark blue winter boots that zipped in the front and was secured by a buckle. They were lined with cream colored wool that, when folded down, would cover the zipper. The boots were cute, but I hoped they fit. Luck must have been on my side because they were my size. *Go me!*

Well, I am dressed, now what? As if someone read my mind, there came a knock on my door. Opening the door, Kimberley was standing there with her brother Knox who looked me up and down. He smiled as I heard Bridget yelling, "What the hell is going on? Who in their right mind gets up this early? No one should be up unless someone is dying or dead!"

Dayton stood in front of her door getting an earful. Walking up to see if I could calm things down, I placed a hand on his shoulder and he turned towards me with a very angry expression. I smiled at him before I looked at Bridget saying, "Well, it is a long drive to London from here, or so I am told. And today is the only day we get to go."

She snapped, "Fine, you go! I'm going back to bed."

Coaxingly, I replied, "Yes, but if I'm remembering right, Dayton told me that Kimberley was going into London to do some shopping. I am sure if you asked her nicely she may let you go with."

In that moment, everyone froze, and I swear a person could have heard the crackling from the candle flames. Then, Bridget stepped out looking at Kimberley asking, "Is this true? You're going shopping?" Kimberley nodded her head as Bridget got a huge smile on her face, before sweetly asking, "May I, pretty please with lots of sugar on top, go with you?"

First anger shot through Kimberley before she gritted out, "I do not see why not."

"Thank you, thank you, thank you! Just give me a couple minutes," she happily said before spinning and closing her door. It made me laugh because it would only take her that long to get ready, especially when shopping was involved. Bridget lives to shop and sometimes the phrase 'shop 'til you drop' was made for anyone who went shopping with her.

Knox walked up saying, "That was impressive."

I cocked my head to look at him. Shaking my head, I laughed, "Not really. I just know that Bridget really loves to shop. I can't tell you how many times I've been dragged with her. I hate it and she loves it. With her, it is always a full day thing and by the time we get back I quite literally come home and drop dead."

Knox laughed, "My sister is the same way." A fully dressed Bridget emerged in an outfit similar to mine, only the top was black and the skirt, yellow. The boots were the same, only in black, and she had them zipped all the way up, while I had mine part way down.

She then grabbed my arm shouting, "Let's get going!" I didn't know why, but I got the impression that Kimberley was pissed off about having to go shopping with Bridget.

Finally, after a long car ride we made it into London. Balin dropped Knox, Dayton, and me at Shakespeare's Globe Theatre, where he had once put on all his plays. It might not have been the original structure, but I was still happy to be seeing it. It turned out we couldn't go in and look around because it was undergoing renovations. At least I got to see the outside, so I was counting it off my checklist.

After standing outside the theatre for a while, Dayton called a taxi to take us to Kensington Gardens. We walked around for a while before coming to the one place I had wanted to see, since I was five, after my dad had read the story of Peter Pan. As the story ended for the one-hundredth time, I told my dad I was going to marry Peter Pan and have Pan babies. He laughed at me, telling me that Peter Pan wasn't real but one day he would take me to London to see Peter Pan's statue. Seeing this Statue was a dream come true that started my tear ducts.

Knox stood next to me, as Dayton stood back, not really interested in anything here. Knox, seeing my tears asked, "Why are you crying?"

I turned to look at him and caught a glimpse of Dayton, who wore a worried expression. Pulling my gaze towards Knox, I smiled saying, "I am crying because I am happy and sad."

Knox handed me a handkerchief for my tears asking, "Why are you happy and sad? I do not understand how a person can be both."

Spinning around to face the statue once more, I laughed. The bronze statue of the boy who would never grow up, surrounded by woodland critters and faeries, warmed my heart. It was like seeing the ending of a Walt Disney fairytale. I never imagined I would actually see the original statue, nor experience England. Some part of me felt like this was all a dream and at any moment I would wake up. Using the cloth for my tears, I answered, "I am happy because I finally get to see the statue of Peter Pan, the boy who will never grow up. I am sad because my dad is not here to see it with me."

Knox laughed, "Well, maybe next time you might get to bring him with you and can see it with him."

I smiled and shook my head, "I can never bring him because he is no longer alive. But, I think he'd be happy I finally got to see the boy I first fell in love with." Turning back to Knox, I smiled, but he looked conflicted as though he didn't know what to say. His expression then turned sour. It was a look I had gotten my whole life, laughing, "Hey, don't worry about it. My dad might not be alive, but he is still here with me because I am alive. So, in a way, he is here too."

He nodded, still looking sour, when Dayton said, "I think it is going to start raining, shall we head to the closest pub?"

My smile widened as I bounced saying, "Oh! That sounds fun! I've never been to one."

The sour expression on Knox's face turned into a mischievous grin as he laughed, "Alright with me."

We entered the pub just as the rain started. Dayton led us to the closest table to the door and sat across from us. I sat on the inside, closest to the clouded window with Knox sitting to my left. Dayton and I sat in silence watching Knox enjoy his beverage. He almost had his drink gone, when I saw the Old Hag from my dreams pacing back and forth. I tried ignoring her scowl, but it was difficult. I could sense her agitated presence the longer I ignored her, because she knew I could see her. As Knox excused himself to find the loo, the old hag came closer. He was a short distance away, the Hag snatched my arm rather tightly, pulling me up off the dark brown, wooden bench and out of the safety of the warm pub. I had been so surprised by the action that I didn't see, nor hear a thing from Knox or Dayton.

I tried to break free of her, but she wouldn't release her tight grasp. Then, I began to beg her to leave me alone, but she wouldn't listen. Before I knew it, she dragged me into a very old broken structure. I was thrown onto a non-existent table and my limbs were belted down. Then, Dayton walked into the structure and froze, a second before Knox. I knew it must have been frightening to see me floating in midair and for no reason.

The Old Hag spoke in a gravelly voice, "I told you to leave! I told you and now you must pay! Just like before!" Horrified, I didn't understand what she was talking about. She pulled out an ax and my fear spiked. I screamed as she started cutting my left arm. Making a quick pass she sliced my legs and cut up my other arm, before she came to my head saying, "Now, it is time to die!"

I screamed at the top of my lungs, shattering her stability as I felt the blade on my throat. Once her energy in this plane, was broken, I fell to the ground bleeding heavily from the cuts she had given me. I couldn't move due to the pain and the terror I felt. Crying from the pain I realized the cuts were in the same place as the ghost in the garden maze.

Dayton walked up to me and knelt down, putting his hand on my head. Before I knew it, I lost all consciousness as the pain left my body. Entering into dreamland, I found myself surrounded by the bliss of nothingness. The black abyss was much better than the active dreams I normally had.

* * *

Sitting in the library, I heard a car door open and close quickly. *That must have been a quick trip into London. Dayton must have wanted to cut it short because he got too annoyed with the mortals.* I heard a commotion and glimpsed several of the medics, who were always kept on staff, run past the open door of the library. Closing my book, I headed to the entrance, only to stop short, as the smell of semi-fresh blood assaulted me. The scent was like heaven; I had never smelled anything as intoxicating. It smelled of honey, sunshine, and a good winter storm all mixed together, and my mouth watered for the taste of the deliciousness. I quickened my pace but stopped as I realized the smell came from Nicole.

She had deep looking cut marks on her arms and legs. I was horrified by the cuts because they were in the same place as my beloved's. The wench did have a small, shallow gash across her neck as if the blade had been stopped before her head was severed. Seeing her in this state brought back the memory of the day my twin soul's body was discovered. *At least this wench still had her head.*

I knew one of my cousins had to lick the wounds to stop the bleeding. The lacerations were deep showing veins, muscle tissue, and bone. I could hear her faint heartbeat and knew she was barely alive. My father and mother walked in asking, "What happened?"

Knox shook his head saying, "I do not know. One moment I was getting up to go to the lavatory and next thing Dayton and I know, Nicole was up and out the pub door. We chased after her into a crumbling building. When we saw her floating in mid-air, we froze, as we did not know what was happening or that she was about to be sliced open. Nicole looked as terrified as we felt and we did not know how to help her. Then, these cuts started forming for no apparent reason. The slicing did not stop until she screamed at the top of her lungs. She can bloody well scream, too! My ears are still ringing." As if to prove a point, he shook them trying to stop the sound.

Goldie came in holding a sleeping Bridget, and she looked less than happy about it. My father asked, "And what happened to her?"

This time, Dayton glared at Bridget's sleeping form answering, "We called Balin to come and get us causing the mortal and Kimberley to cut their shopping trip short. After seeing Nicole in this state, Bridget freaked. She hyperventilated until she fainted. Goldie, can you take Bridget up to her room? She should be waking up soon."

Goldie headed up the stairs, carrying an unconscious Bridget. She paused when she saw me, "Too bad you hate witches. I think you would get along better with Nicole, than this twat." At that, everyone's eyes turned towards me and I shrugged like it was no big deal. However, my heart ached painfully the longer I stared at the wench's unconscious body. *This is crazy! I already lost the girl I loved, and I should not be feeling anything for some pathetic mortal.*

But, what if one of these girls is the reincarnation of my twin soul? It would explain why I never lost my mind. No, it is not possible. I should not think about such things because it will only make me more depressed than I already am. I need a distraction. Right on cue, one of my mother's chamber maids passed and I knew exactly what I needed, a fix. What better fix is there than that of the sexual kind? Working my magic on the naive girl, she fell for my charms.

She then mumbled, "Asshole," as she angrily picked up her clothes and pulled them on. I laid in bed thinking. *I could care less if she was stupid enough to think I actually wanted her. It was not my fault I helped her to lose her virginity. She should have done what others normally do and ignore me. I always enjoy taking a Cimmerian's virginity. There are no complications, like with mortals.*

I laughed, "Sweetheart, what did you actually expect from me? I just needed a fix and you were there. Not my fault you made the wrong assumption."

Throwing her shirt back on she said, "Yeah, well I cannot wait until the day you actually find your twin soul and lose her because of your high and mighty arrogance."

I laughed, "You are not the first to say that to me, sweetheart, and you will not be the last." With that, she huffed out of my room and headed back to do her job.

I had gotten out of bed and put my boxers on when my father and mother came in looking angry and disappointed once again. With a sigh, I asked, "What have I done now to get that look?"

My father yelled, "You know damn well what you did and after we warned you! Dayton has even warned you and you still go and do it."

"I had an itch and I had a little help in scratching it. It is better than killing one of the mortals," I replied.

My mother screeched, "You had an itch? Is that the only excuse you can come up with? Your father and cousin have warned you! Now, I will be the one to serve you the punishment."

Laughing, I dryly said, "And what punishment could you serve, that would be worse than being cursed to remain for eternity in this bloody castle?"

This time she laughed, "I am going to have everyone removed from this castle except for the male guards, the two mortals, and your cousin Knox."

At that I froze, not sure what to say or do, but slowly my anger overtook me. Eyes pooling with blood, I snapped, "Do you want me to kill them or something?! Or do you just want me to lose what little I have left of my mind?!"

They did not say anything as they left. *Are my parents insane? Do they really want me gone that much?* I was once again seeing red, and I heard a soft heartbeat that I wanted and I wanted it now. I quickly ran towards the sound and found myself in Nicole's room. Quickly, I ran to her and threw her hair to the side. My fangs popped out seeing her pulsating artery, but I could not strike. I could not drain the life from her.

I had never felt such guilt as I did in that one moment and I did not understand why. Nicole was a simple-minded mortal. She was curvy and plain, however, there was something about her, that I doubt anybody had ever cherished. She felt like the kind of girl that needed to be shielded, but no one had ever protected her from anything. My fangs retracted, and I pulled away as tears fell from my eyes. *I have finally lost my marbles.*

I had never been an emotional person and only cried once in my whole life. To be crying for no reason at all did not make any sense. Wiping the light blue tears away, I left Nicole's room and headed to my spot in the library. *I hope reading my book will help get my thoughts free of Nicole and the confusion I have towards her.*

CHAPTER 13

The Imprisonment

I hadn't been able to get out of bed for the last few days because my body hurt so bad and felt weak. Dayton had come in a lot throughout the day to help me eat or to go to the bathroom, which was a bit awkward for me, but nice all the same. Knox came in some, too. Both said they wanted to make sure I was getting better and wasn't feeling too lonely.

Bridget came in at the end of the day, before she went off to bed. She talked about everything she and Stan had done all day. A lot of it sounded fun to me, but Bridget thought it was boring and talked more about how she wanted to rip his clothes off and ravish him. It wasn't something I wanted to hear about, but it was typical Bridget. She told me about their steamy make-out sessions and that he kissed better than any guy she had ever been with. This made her believe he would be a wiz in the sack.

After five days in bed, I was glad to finally be medically cleared to get up and out of my room. Slowly getting out of bed, I made my way to the wardrobe. I had to rest on the fainting couch, due to dizziness, before opening the wardrobe doors. I was super bummed because all the beautiful gowns were gone and replaced with today's British fashion. After going through the clothes, I decided on a knitted, brown-checked sweatshirt that had pink and red stripes intertwining and a pair of dark blue jeans that flared at the bottom. There were a bunch of shoes along the base of the wardrobe. I picked out a pair of teal ankle boots with a belt that buckled on the outside of the leg.

It took me longer than normal to get dressed because I changed sitting on the couch. As I finished Dayton and Knox came in with breakfast. They both took a step into my room and stared at me. Knox looked surprised and Dayton looked angry and worried. Wanting to see them smile, I smiled saying, "Look! I am feeling much better today. I even got myself dressed."

This got Knox to laugh, "We can see that, but it is a good thing my sister is not here because she would totally strip you down and dress you properly."

I frowned looking down, asking, "Do I look bad?"

Dayton came and set food on the coffee table, "No, you do not look bad. The shoe color does not match the outfit, is all. Kimberley likes things to flow together and the shoes prevent that."

"Oh…" was all I could muster because I didn't know what else to say. Color coordination was the one thing Bridget tried and failed to help me with. She says, with love, that I am a walking fashion disaster. *I can't help that I am fashion challenged.*

Knox sat on the opposite side of the coffee table, as Dayton sat next to me. Knox watched me eat the toast and porridge as Dayton seemed to be looking everywhere else. When I was almost finished, Knox asked, "Nicole, what would you like to do today?"

I looked at him uncertainly because I hadn't really thought much about it. Letting his question roll around in my brain for a few, I remembered something Bridget told me. Biting on my bottom lip, I thought about nearly being killed by a vengeful spirit and decided to grow a vagina. Determined, I asked, "Well, Bridget shared with me how she and Stan went riding on horses. It has been something I have wanted to try since I was little but was too scared. Is that a possibility?" The last part I said in a quiet, uncertain voice.

Dayton wrapped his arm around me asking, "You have never been riding before?"

"No, I have always been too scared to get on or near one," I answered.

Knox then stood up and happily said, "Then, we shall take you trail riding. However, you will have to ride with Dayton, as I am not as experienced a rider as him. Is that ok?"

I nodded my head and noticed how Dayton looked like he didn't care a bit about riding with me. It hurt a little and I didn't understand why he would be acting this way.

Sensing Dayton's tension, Knox laughed, "Alright, how about we head to the barn and get the horses ready to go?" We all stood up and slowly made our way out to the stables.

Once we got there, I found a tall stool to rest on while they readied the horses. Dayton pulled out a black horse that had a white patch on its chest, and a white four-leaf clover on its forehead. He put her reins on and tied her to a post, before going and getting a beautiful multi-colored horse. This one was mostly white, with black, brown, and grey spots. After putting on the reins he tied him to a different post. He then took a saddle from Knox and they each placed one on their horse and cinched it up.

Once the saddles were on, Knox came over, as Dayton rechecked the saddles to make sure they were secured saying, "All right. The black horse's name is Clover and you will be riding her with Dayton. The painted one is Paxton whom I will be riding. Clover is better with new riders, while Paxton likes to gallop." I nodded my head gulping because I couldn't believe that I was about to get on my first horse ever.

I guess the guys heard my gulp, as they both laughed. Dayton chuckled, "Do not worry. Clover and I will take good care of you. Right girl?" As he uncharacteristically cooed the last part, I started to feel more at ease. Knox helped me off the stool and brought me over to Dayton and Clover. Dayton lifted me up into the saddle before untying the reins and hopping on behind me. "Ummm, shouldn't I be behind you... not in front?" I inquired, befuddled by the close proximity of his body.

He had us walk around in a circle before answering, "It is to make sure you do not fall off. Your body is still recovering, and I do not want you to sustain any more injuries." I nodded my head as we found a trail that was well hidden behind the back of the barn.

It was a rather nice day. Knox had told me Paxton enjoyed running and moments after we started on the trail they took off at a dead sprint. *Paxton must really not like to walk.* As Dayton and I walked in silence, I finally decided to ask him, "Hey, Dayton. I am curious about something. Why do I get the feeling that at times you enjoy my company, while other times you would rather be anywhere else?"

He sighed, "You noticed, huh?"

I laughed, nodding, "Uh huh." Dayton seemed to answer questions with a question. It was annoying, but it seemed like his way of not telling me the answer.

Again, he sighed, "I suppose you want an explanation, right?" I nodded, and he continued, "Well, I feel like I can be myself with you, while I cannot be myself with others. My life is complicated, and I do not want to get too close and end up hurting you."

I thought about that and concluded he was already in a relationship. *Great! I start to like a relatively good guy and of course he's taken. Just my luck!* I decided to laugh, "So... who is she? I don't think you could hurt me as I don't go for the unattainable, but I kind of considered us becoming... friends?"

He abruptly stopped the horse. Confused, I turned to see a sad look on his face before it turned into regret. Clover started walking again as I faced forward. He sadly said, "Her name is Enya O'Shea. Our parents put us in an arranged marriage before either of us were born. She is alright, but she was not my choice... if I had one."

"I'm sorry," I said, then asked out of morbid curiosity, "If you could pick what type of girl would you choose?"

We paused again for a brief moment, before he answered, "Well, I want to be in love with the girl before I marry her. I did once before, a long time ago. She was much like you, but was very sick. She died before I could back out of my arranged marriage, with Enya."

I started sobbing. I could never imagine experiencing anything like that. I could only imagine how it must have felt to lose the one person that you loved more than anything. He stopped Clover once more, "Hey, no need for you to cry about it. It was not in my stars."

Hiccupping, I said, "I know, but it's wrong. Two people who love each other should be allowed to be together and it doesn't seem fair." He sighed, lifted me up and turned me around in the saddle, so I was facing him. He then wrapped his arms around me, letting me cry into him.

Once I had calmed down a bit, he said, "Thank you for crying for me, but it really is not necessary. I did not even cry over it, so it probably was not true love. Maybe more of a love-lust relationship."

When I was about to reply, my entire body went rigid as everything around me disappeared and a fog started to roll in around me. Dayton faded away and I no longer sat on Clover. Instead, I was standing and starting to get really scared. Spinning around, looking for the spirit responsible for this, I spotted a girl about fifteen years old, who floated into my line of sight.

She was all grey and white, but pretty in a sickly sort of way. The girl stood about my height, with plump, thin girly lips, pronounced cheekbones, a slender button nose, a thin stick figured body, with no breasts to speak of. It was obvious to me that she must have died before she had developed into a woman. The girl walked up to me and placed her hand on my stomach. A bright light shot from her hand, into me. With this motion, the fog that surrounded us cleared and I felt a warmth growing in my lower abdomen.

Looking up at my shocked face, she said, "What was once taken has been restored. My mother should have never committed the crimes she has done. I need to fix her mistakes. I will protect you from here on, but there is someone that still threatens you. Trust Athelstan, Knox, and Dayton to keep you safe, but not all the guards will keep you out of harm's way. Now, you must hurry! Your friend needs you! Tell Dae to take you back in Cimmerian speed to your friend's room!"

Before I could ask her a single question, the darkness was gone. Soon, light filtered through and I was staring at a worried Dayton. Blinking a few times, I had an uncontrollable urge to find Bridget. Looking at Dayton I said, "I need to find someone named Dae."

Dayton completely froze before he growled, "How do you know that name?"

I shook my head saying, "The girl told me. She said I needed to get to my friend and to tell somebody named Dae to use their Cimmerian speed to take me to her room. I don't know what a Cimmerian is, but if they can help, I don't care."

Dayton got off Clover as Knox came back to us. Pulling me off, he handed the reins to Knox, growling, "I need to take Nicole back to the castle, fast. Take Clover back to the barn and have Ted tend to the horses. Then, you need to come to Bridget's room as fast as you can." Knox looked perplexed but nodded. Dayton then picked me up bridal style, saying, "Close your eyes or you may get sick."

Closing my eyes, I squeaked, "Okay." After a few seconds, I opened them and was stunned to find myself back in the castle looking at a very scared and angry Dayton. I followed his gaze and froze. It looked exactly like my dream, except Bridget was naked and Stan was half naked, lying on top of her body.

As the shock wore off, I squirmed out of Dayton's hold, only to fall onto the floor with a loud thud. Jumping to my feet, I ran over to Stan and Bridget. Not really sure what to do, something told me to press really hard on his Adam's apple. Quickly, following my gut, I pushed hard on his throat with my fingers causing him to groan and release his fangs from Bridget's neck. *What the hell??! Fangs?! Don't vampires have fangs?* He still had her blood on his lips and teeth. I froze, seeing this. Dayton at that moment threw Stan clear across the room. Stan slumped to the floor, only to growl as he stood up quicker than my eyes could follow. Dayton took a stance between Bridget, me, and Stan. His objective was to keep us safe.

Bridget moaned which drew my attention to her. I saw the bite mark on her neck heal over instantly. *What the hell?! Is this even possible?* I then heard a voice telling me that I needed to get Bridget out of the castle and out of England. *Alright… easier said than done because I know Bridget would not leave without me.*

Then, I heard Stan growl, "Dayton... this is none of your's or that Seer's business! You both need to move, now!"

Dayton growled back, "No! I will not! You are angry and thirsty! You will kill your last chance."

Ok wait… last chance for what? What the hell is going on around here?

"I do not care, Dayton! You need to get used to the idea that you are going to be the next King and stay out of my way," Stan yelled, as his eyes started to glow a deep, deep red turning a black color. He started to look more demonic, than a human being.

"Move Nicole! Move in front of Dayton now and make a deal for your friend's freedom! You have to do it now Nicole, or it will be too late," a familiar female voice said in my head.

As Stan moved, I did as the voice said and surprised both him, as well as Dayton. I yelled, "Stan! You will not kill my friend!"

Stan went rigid and said, "Alright, I will not kill your friend."

"Good," I snapped, nodding. *Wait… what?! Was it that easy?*

"No, it is not that easy," the voice said once more, *"look."*

Frowning, I thought, *Look at what?* Looking at Stan, I saw that nothing had changed in his eyes. They were the same demonic color. I heard Bridget try to move from the bed. Turning around, I watched as she fell to the floor. Dayton quickly grabbed her, trying to hold her still, but she was squirming too much.

"Tell him you will stay here with him and do whatever he wants! Tell him you give him your body and soul," the voice yelled at me!

What? No! I won't do that. I won't give that asshole my body or soul, I angrily thought.

"Then, lose your friend," the voice snapped.

Dayton then shouted, "Athelstan! Release her and I will take you to the kitchen for something to drink!"

Stan growled, "No! I want it fresh and I want it from that lying, cheating, horny tart." At that moment, I knew he was serious about killing my friend and I was the only one who could save her.

I took in a deep breath and stepped towards Stan, as Dayton yelled at me to stay away. Knox, Kimberley, and Stan's parents came into the room. Staring him right in the eyes, as tears began to fall, I said, "Stan… let my best friend go home to the U.S. You can have my body and soul to do as you wish."

Everyone gasped, and Stan froze before he sank his fangs into my neck. It hurt, but after a second there was no pain… nothing. It felt like it was the right thing to happen, almost like I was born for this moment, right here. My eyelids slowly fluttered closed as I passed out.

* * *

I have spent the last five days with this annoying little tart and I was about to lose it. She had me passed the point of drinking from her. Now, I also had the need to screw her into oblivion. Today, we had spent the day in the gaming room and she played the *I have never played this game before… can you show me how?* It was something new that no other mortal had ever tried with me before. I found it quite amusing, but I could not get the tart out of my head. *I swear, if she does not stop thinking about all those sexual fantasies, I am going to take her and then kill her.*

Out of the corner of my eye I saw Knox, Dayton, and Nicole walk slowly by the gaming room door. When I heard the back door open and close, a wicked thought crossed my mind. I planted a slow, soft kiss on the tart's neck sending a shiver down her spine. It was what she had been waiting for, for days now. I smiled as I wrapped my arms around her waist seductively saying, "Since your friend is no longer bed ridden, how about we go to your room and tinker about a bit, while we have a chance?" She did not say a word, but grabbed my hand, pulling me out of the room, towards hers. I was quite happy with myself, as I was going to sate both of my needs. *As long as no one interrupts us, I shall finally rid myself of this annoying mortal once and for all.*

Once we entered her room and the door closed, she had me pushed up against the door. Our lips mingled for a while until she pulled back saying, "You are too clothed." The tart started unbuttoning my top before moving to my pants. *She must really want this more than I do.*

Before I knew it, we were on her bed and she had somehow stripped herself down to only her bra and matching thong. Smiling, I let my hands and lips work their magic and soon she was ready for me. However, I no longer wanted to screw her, I only wanted her blood. Her nice, warm, fresh blood sounded more pleasing than sex, in and of itself. I knew my thirst had to do with the new moon than with anything else. My fangs popped out and sank into her neck with ease, as she let out a pleasurable moan.

After a couple of minutes, I felt a pressure on my throat, causing me to stop and pull back. I turned to look at the person who dared to interrupt my meal. I spotted Nicole standing there with a look of horror. I growled at her. *How dare she stop me from feeding off her friend?*

When I was about to launch myself at her, Dayton threw me across the room and into the far wall, beside the wardrobe. Quickly standing up, I faced Dayton as he took a fighting stance between me and my meals.

I growled, "Dayton, this is none of yours, nor that Seer's business! You both need to move, now!"

He had the insolence to growl back, "No! I will not! You are angry and thirsty! You will kill your last chance!" I almost laughed because I did not have a chance in hell of freeing myself from this curse. These two pathetic mortals were not going to save my worthless arse, no matter what the Old Hag said.

"I do not care Dayton! You need to get used to the idea that you are going to be the next King! Stay out of my way," I yelled at him because he seriously needed to get used to it!

As I moved to throw my cousin out of my way, Nicole moved in front of him. It surprised both of us, but it also made us very angry; I was angry because I wanted my cousin out of my way. He was ticked because he was trying to keep her safe from me. She then yelled, "Stan! You will not kill my friend!"

I went ridged to that, "Alright, I will not kill your friend." What the hell was I saying? I was going to kill the little tart, then I was going to kill this little virgin here for getting in my way.

"Good," she snapped nodding. *Good? We will see about that.* I fixed my gaze on the semi-conscious tart and easily broke into her head, commanding her to come to me.

Nicole turned around as her friend moved from the bed, only to watch her fall onto the floor. Dayton quickly grabbed the tart, trying to hold her still, but she was squirming far too much. He struggled to keep her safe from me. Dayton then shouted, "Athelstan! Release her and I will take you to the kitchen for something to drink!"

I do not want that warmed up crap! I want fresh blood. Blood from a mortal body and I want it from these two. I then growled, "No! I want it fresh and I want it from that lying, cheating, horny tart."

Nicole took in a deep breath as she took a step towards me. Dayton yelled at her to stay away from me, but his words seemed lost on her. As she stared right into my eyes, her tears began to fall. Then I heard the door fly open as she said, "Stan... let my best friend go home to the U.S. You can have my body and soul to do as you wish."

I heard a bunch of gasps, as I froze for a brief moment, before I sank my fangs into her neck, tasting ambrosia. I pulled her closer, to drink her blood deeply, before I released her. Pulling her motionless body away from me, I let her fall to the floor, horrified by the fact that I bit her and the sensation that I must now follow what she had proposed.

Dayton had managed to catch her before she hit the ground. All around me I heard people screaming and yelling, however, none of their words made it into my mind. The need to get away from this girl grew to an epic proportion, as I quickly ran to my favorite spot.

CHAPTER 14

The Old Tradition

It had been a few days since I nearly killed the mortal tart and imprisoned the seer. My parents sent Goldie to escort Bridget back home and modified the mortal's memory. Goldie was instructed to erase all traces of Nicole's life.

Nicole had been asleep for the last two days and in that time, my parents had the wench and all of her belongings moved into my room. I was the least bit thrilled about it. Since the wench had been in my room, I took up residence in the library. I went back only to shower and change clothes.

Dayton had not left her side and refused to acknowledge me. He seemed really pissed off about something and I could not figure out what. My parents and the other guards were worried about him, as well. No one could figure out why she proposed giving me her body and soul to do with as I wished. *I want nothing to do with her, but my body seems to have a claim on her and it truly pisses me off. Every time I go into my room, I see Dayton holding onto her body and I involuntarily growl. He only looks at me to glare and growl back, flashing his fangs. It is truly grating on my last nerves because I do not understand what my deal is.*

Meals had been silent as my parents also refused to talk to me. Kimberley did not know what to say. Knox had become abnormally silent, which was strange, because he normally did not let things get him down. Dayton was absent from the table taking his meals in *my* room. Knox went to my room every now and then to check and see how Nicole was doing. Dayton would answer his questions, but only if I was not around, otherwise they both remained silent in my presence.

Sitting at the end of the table, I finally had enough. Slamming my fist down, I snapped, "Alright! Get it over and done with because this silence is getting old and on my last nerve!"

My father looked up at me and growled, "Do you have any idea what is going on? Or what you have done to that girl?"

"Dad, it is not that big of a deal. I bit her, big whoop," I said. *It really is not that big of a deal as Cimmerians need blood on occasion. It is not as though I killed her.*

He stood up yelling, "Not a big deal! Not a big Deal! That girl is becoming a Cimmerian Shade now because of you! You are married to her and if by some miracle she survives you are still going to be married to her! The marriage is not something that can be annulled, and you cannot get divorced! You are married to her until death do you part and if one of you dies, so does the other! And what is more *Son* she is not your true love, therefore, she has not broken the curse! The curse is still in place! We can feel it! You have not only botched this for yourself, you have now blundered that girl into your mess!"

I sat there stunned. *How could I honestly be married to that mortal? How could she be turning into a Cimmerian Shade? I did not release any of my venom into her, so how is that even possible?* Frowning, I calmly asked, "Father, how are we married? We did not have any sort of ceremony?"

My father's jaw tightened, and his fists clenched as he said, "When she said '...you can have my body and soul to do as you wish.' She unknowingly said the words to an old Shade ritual for a marriage ceremony and you completed that ritual when you bit her. In that old ritual, if the bride or groom is mortal and is bitten by a Shade, their body goes into a comatose state until they are completely turned."

My mother then placed her hand on my father's arm, softly saying, "Eldon, it is not their fault. Neither of them knew of the old customs, but it is odd how she knew the words to say to invoke it. None of the eighth generation knows of the ritual and it is not something our kind have told mortals. Son, this is much more serious than you simply being married to her, or her turning into a Cimmerian Shade. You are going to start to feel things for her. For example, the inexplicable need to always be by her side and the jealousy you will feel towards any male, that so much as talks to her. You will not be able to control other urges that will come because you were never taught how to handle them."

That explains why I do not like Dayton being so close to Nicole. What other urges will I have that I do not already? I am already a sex maniac and lust after fresh mortal blood. I cannot take the heated canned blood, nor the nasty animal rubbish. What can be worse than that?

Standing up, I left the dining hall and headed to my favorite spot to process this new information. *None of it makes sense and is impossible to believe. I cannot really be married to the stupid wench and I know I did not turn her. They are both being worry warts, when it is not necessary. Hmmm, if that is the case then I do not need to dwell on this and they can continue the silent treatment.*

* * *

When I woke up, I had a burning sensation in my throat, which meant I was coming down with a cold. I hated colds and being sick; it was the worst feeling in the whole wide world. I always got so tired and exhausted that it weakened my ability to suppress my foresight. Usually, I ended up bed ridden for a few weeks and was once institutionalized for insanity. Being sick was not an option. This time, though, I felt bruised and sore all over, which confused me as I normally didn't feel sore when sick.

Opening my eyes, I saw Dayton lying next to me. He smiled and placed his hand on my face, rubbing it in a gentle manor, before asking, "How are you feeling?"

Confused, I replied, "Fine, but my throat hurts. I think I'm coming down with something."

Moving a strand of hair, he got up looking sad, saying, "I can get you something for your throat. Wait here." After he left, I sat up and was surprised to find myself in a different room. This room had a lot of dark furniture in it. The bed on which I laid, was a dark brown, four-poster bed. Unlike my old room, there were no curtains and on either side of the frame was a black night stand. The bed faced a door, and along the right side rested a plain, black wardrobe with a matching dresser on the opposite wall. Next to the wardrobe, and closest to me, was another door which, I assumed, led to a chamber pot. The only similarity to my room were the candles that lit up the dark interior.

After absorbing my new surroundings, Dayton came back in, followed by Knox and Eldon. Dayton held a glass of a dark looking milkshake and

I figured the coolness of it would help my throat. He walked over and climbed up onto the bed next to me, passing me the drink. Drinking it, I found that it wasn't cold, but rather warm. Frowning, I asked, "Dayton, what is this?"

He rolled his eyes and said, "Just drink it. I promise it will help your throat."

Frowning at the drink, I decided it might be best to listen. The moment the warm liquid touched my tongue, a sensation, not like anything I had ever experienced before, exploded on my taste buds. It tasted like chocolate, peanut butter, banana, and mint all rolled into one. After I finished the beverage, I licked my lips and realized that it helped my throat. It made the soreness go away completely. "Wow, that was really good! What was it?"

Eldon then sat at the end of the bed, looking rather serious, saying, "Nicole, you do not want to know the answer quite yet, alright…. I do have a question for you and I need an honest answer, ok?"

Confused, I nodded my head saying, "Alright, shoot."

He sighed, asking, "Why did you tell my son that if he let your friend go, he could have your body and soul to do as he wished?"

I frowned, "Well, the voice, I sometimes hear in my head, was screaming at me and instructed me to say those words. The voice has never been wrong before, and it told me that if I did not say them, I would lose my best friend forever. I would rather her be alive, than dead, and I knew if I didn't do anything, that is what would have happened. Before Dayton carried me into Bridget's room, I saw a girl on the trail who told me to find someone named *Dae* and have him take me *at Cimmerian speed* to her room. I think the girl knew what Stan was about to do and wanted me to stop him. She also said something her mother did, she had to set right and what was once taken is now undone; whatever that means…."

Stan's father looked shocked, before turning thoughtful, asking, "What do you mean a girl you saw before?"

Oh no, I shouldn't have said that. Now I have to answer. Biting on my bottom lip, I nervously replied, "Well, for some reason since coming here, it's like…. Wait, I should probably start at the beginning….

"When I turned thirteen I started to see the dead. Ghosts, trapped souls, spirits, whatever you want to call them. When I discovered my abilities, I was living with a nice, religious family and they believed that the devil was inside me. They proceeded to have me exorcised, which went on for weeks. It was not until I played along, acting out the possession, that they accepted the demon's exile. I missed so much school from the exorcism that I was quickly removed from their house. I ended up hospitalized due to my weakness from starvation....

"After that, I decided it was best that I did not tell anybody about my gifts and I learned to block them out. It annoyed some ghosts and the more violent ones became so angry that they lashed out at me. Ever since I came here, it is like my ability to block them out has diminished. They just come in whenever they please. The Old Hag, who I've been seeing in my dreams since we arrived, was the scariest. Especially, when she used that axe to cut and slice me, in that decrepit, old building in London. I was glad when I was able to shake her hold on this plane, before she cut off my head." I shivered at the thought of that, before continuing, "The girl in the garden, that was bleeding from her neck, was creepy. I liked the girl that I saw when horseback riding. She seemed nice, but very confusing." I shook my head, because I still didn't know what she was talking about, or who *Dae* was.

Knox sat next to his uncle and reached out to touch my hand saying, "Nicole, that must have been so awful. I am truly sorry for what you have seen here."

I laughed, "It's alright. It is just a part of me. I cannot change that, and I have learned to accept it for what it is."

When I was about to ask them a question, I felt something weird in the pit of my stomach. It was like something moved, but maybe I needed to use the bathroom. Pushing myself over to the edge of the bed, Dayton followed my movement. Heading to the chamber pot, with him following close behind me, I turned and snapped, "Are you going to follow me into the bathroom?!"

He looked shocked, as did everyone else, including myself. I had never snapped at anyone before and that was no good reason to shout. Once again, I felt the odd movement and it did not feel like I needed to use the bathroom. It felt like something was *inside* of me. Dayton looked sad, saying, "I wanted to make sure you got there alright, without falling down or passing out. Your body is still much too weak."

Feeling the motion once more, I closed the distance between Dayton and myself. Moving his hand over my stomach he stared at me confused, asking, "Nicole, what are…" he didn't finish his sentence. Whatever he was about to say halted when he felt the weird sensation. Fear crossed his face, before he got on his knees and placed his ear to my stomach. Looking up at me he asked, "How?"

"How, what?" I didn't quite understand what was going on in my stomach. I'd never felt anything like it before. I'd felt hunger, constipation, cramps, even pain from my pancreatitis, but I had never felt my stomach jerk like this.

"Nicole, you are pregnant." Dayton whispered low to me, in disbelief. Feeling the movement once more, I could not believe it. *I am pregnant? That isn't possible. Virgins can't become pregnant and I'm not the Virgin Mary.*

Eldon and Knox got off the bed, confused. Eldon then asked, "Dayton, what is wrong? Why are you listening to Nicole's stomach?"

Dayton stood up and pulled me towards Eldon. As I had done with him, he placed his uncle's hand on my stomach. After a few moments, my stomach moved once more, and fear crossed his face as well. He then demanded, "Tell me everything that happened with the girl that told you to find Dae!"

Frowning, I said, "Well, there was a black abyss around me, that slowly started to fill up with fog. The girl appeared and walked up to me. She placed her hand on my stomach and a bright light shot from her hand. It cleared out all the fog that had surrounded us and then she said, 'What was once taken has been restored. My mother should have never committed the crimes she has done. I need to fix her mistakes. Trust Athelstan, Knox, and Dayton to keep you safe, but not all the guards will keep you out of harm's way.'"

At that moment, Stan came into the bedroom, with an angry expression on his face. He quickly ran over and threw his dad and cousins away from me. Stan then began to growl, rather aggressively, as the three of them slumped on the floor. Then, my inner voice said, *"Place your hand on him and tell him that it is alright."*

Confused, I thought, *how come?*

"Because if you do not, he will kill his family to keep them from you," the voice said, as I began to realize that I had heard that voice recently but couldn't place where.

"Trust me. He will kill them because he has not yet gotten control of his new emotions. He has not accepted the truth and needs time," the voice said.

Ok, I thought, reaching my hand out to touch Stan's arm. He flinched at my touch, but when he turned toward me I couldn't help but smile, saying, "Stan, it is alright." Stan stared at me for a long time, but he then moved his hand to my stomach and tears fell from his eyes. I did not understand why he was crying, but when I was about to say something to comfort him, he left as quickly as he came. He left me there, feeling sad and alone, which did not make any sense. Although, nothing made sense anymore, and for the first time in a long time, I collapsed. I couldn't breathe and my heart hurt. It felt worse than when I found my dad dead on our bathroom floor. *Why do I feel this way?*

I couldn't see anything through my tears, but I knew someone came in through the door. They ran over and wrapped their arms around me, saying, "Shh... Nicole, it is going to be alright. Everything will be fine." I knew then, that it was Stan's mother by her voice. I felt like nothing was ever going to be the same again. She held me as I sobbed, trying to soothe me, but it didn't help. I cried myself to sleep in her arms.

* * *

I cannot believe I threw my dad and cousins like that, nor can I believe I was seriously planning on killing them.... All over some girl.... A girl that I cannot stand? Why the hell did I place my hand on her stomach like that and then cry? What scares me more is the need to kiss her.... I should not want to kiss her and even now my body is demanding that I go back to her. There is this feeling that she needs me.... Well... I do not care if she needs me. I want nothing to do with her and I refuse to believe any of that nonsense my parents were spewing about the old ritual and us being married....

I am not married to her and I cannot believe that they are forcing me to share my room with her.... It is my room; my personal space and I should not have to share it with her of all people.... That is, it! My parents can be mad at me all they want, but I want nothing to do with Nicole. Nicole can sleep in my room and I will find somewhere else to sleep.... I will ignore her whenever we end up in the same room, that way I can finally die in peace. That will work out for the best and then Dayton will take over as King and the curse will have finally ended me.

I then plopped myself on my favorite seat in the library, rather pleased with my decision because it could not fail. It was fail proof. *I am good at ignoring people and I am good at giving the cold shoulder. That is what I am going to do, give Nicole the cold shoulder.* Tears swelled in my eyes again.

Bloody-hell! This happened when I had placed my hand on her stomach. What made me touch her stomach?... I did not ask for this... I did not ask for any of it! She was the one who invoked the old tradition, not me! She should suffer the consequences.... Then, why do I feel like I have a big hole in my chest? It feels as though my chest is lonely or rather it makes me feel lonely. I am not lonely, and I do not need that girl... I do not need anyone.... Not my parents, not my cousin's, and especially not Nicole! I am better off alone because then I will hurt less people when I finally die. Laughing at this, I realized how Shakespeare had gotten it correct in his plays with tragic endings. My life had been nothing, but one big tragedy.

CHAPTER 15

The Truth

Stan had not spoken to me since he tossed his Dad and cousins into the wall. I could not help but feel as though I had done something wrong, but I did not know what. His mother brought an on-staff, female doctor to check up on me and the mystery baby. The woman was concerned about the baby and would not tell me anything, but informed Stan's parents of everything. Corliss would only tell me that it was going to be alright, but I could see worry in her eyes.

I had not seen Dayton or Knox in the last few days, either. In fact, all the men in this place stayed away from me. If they saw me, they would turn around, leaving quickly. If that was not bad enough, Kimberley and a guard named Goldie were always with me. Everywhere I went, they went. Whatever I did, they did it with me. It was driving me crazy.

On top of that, when Goldie got back from taking Bridget home, she had all of my belongings with her. I do mean all of my stuff, too. All my clothes, my costumes, my few shoes, my stuffed animals, my pictures and photo books, my CD's, my DVD's, my VHS's, my TV, my VCR, my DVD player, my books, both my Kindles, my blankets, my sheets, my pillow... everything I owned she brought back and I did not understand why. Why did they have all my stuff brought over to England? I knew that I was stuck here, but Stan had to let me leave at some point, as my life was back home in the States.

At the moment, I was in Stan's bed trying to go to sleep but could not. One reason being, I had a feeling that if I did, I would see something. I didn't want to see anything, or anybody. The second reason was my mind kept racing. It felt like a race car driving on a track. It would not shut off. If I tapped my finger, or my foot, the racing stopped, but sleep still eluded me. Finally, I gave up and shoved myself out of bed. I then walked outside and to the garden.

The sky was clear, and I could see the moon and stars. It lit up the garden maze, making it seem magical. Soon, I came to the spot where I heard the scream. The open circle was even more beautiful at night. As I was walking around the statue, a hand fell on my shoulder, making me jump and scream. Spinning around, I saw the girl from my vision, while riding with Dayton. She looked the same, but sad in a way.

With an apologetic voice, she said, "I am sorry, I scared you. That was not my intention."

"It's alright. What is it you want, this time," I asked?

She smiled and then the scary Old Hag from before came out of the dark, blood coating her, but I knew it was not her own. I started to step backwards, but the girl grabbed me saying, "It is alright, my Mamma, Luella, will not harm you. I asked her to come because you can show her the truth; the truth of my past and the real reason why I died."

Tears welled up in my eyes, but I nodded my head yes. It was then that I heard Dayton and Eldon shouting my name. I closed my eyes breaking down my walls. Dayton and Eldon found me as my gift became unblocked and blackness took over. I saw Dayton grab me before my body collapsed.

The old woman, Luella, and the girl were there with me, as our surroundings changed. We were still at the castle, but everything was shorter and smaller in the garden. The girl was walking with a much younger Goldie. Goldie then said in a Scottish accent, "Lady Maida, why do you smile so?"

Maida replied, "I smile so, because I am in love."

"That is the most wondrous news. Have you told anybody yet? Who is the lucky guy?" Goldie asked.

Maida shook her head saying, "No, you are the first, but as to whom, I wish to not tell. We both wish to keep it secret." Goldie never said anything else and the scene changed once more.

Dayton was there and he too, looked much younger. He looked worried and was pacing. When an ill looking Maida walked in, Dayton quickly ran up to her and lifted her into his arms kissing her passionately. They were in an empty hallway and he then sat back against the wall with Maida sitting between his legs. His hand moved slowly up and down her side.

For the longest time, neither said a word until Maida asked, "Were you able to convince your dad to marry for love, Dae?"

Dayton was Dae! He then sighed, "No, he will not budge. He said it was agreed on before we were born and I cannot back out now."

She sighed and turned to look at him saying, "Then I, Maida Avis Miller, give you Dayton Harvard Moren my heart, my soul, and my body to do with as you see fit." Dayton groaned and his fangs grew out, before sinking into Maida's neck. Both their bodies glowed a dark red color. Then the scene changed to Maida and Dayton naked in a bed.

Luella took in a deep breath. Things fast forwarded, and Maida was standing in front of an altar. I was not sure what she was doing, but she was chanting something. After she had finished, Dayton ran in and grabbed a pale looking Maida.

Dayton then yelled, "Maida what did you do?"

"I freed you to marry Lady Enya Lynn O'Shea. Your father finally gets what he wants, and you can be with the one you truly love," she said crying.

"I love you, not her. Why would ye do such a thing," he asked? She did not say anything and collapsed. Grabbing her he shouted, "Mia, Mia!"

Luella came in and ran to her daughter asking, "Dayton, what happened? What is wrong with her?"

Dayton could not say a word; he just held on to her. Finally, Maida gasping, "You were wrong mom! I will never find my true love. He does not exist." Then, she stopped breathing and Dayton began to shake her. Her mother left with a horrified, pained, and angry expression. The scene then changed to nothing, but blackness.

I was confused and turned to Maida asking, "I don't understand. What was all that? None of that made a lick of sense to me."

Luella then said, "It was not meant for you to understand. It was meant for me."

"Mamma, you need to let the child's soul go now. She needs to have it or the baby will die," Maida said.

My hands went to my stomach protectively, asking, "What do you mean, or *my baby will die?*"

Maida then sighed, "Nicole, the reason the doctor keeps coming to check on you is because your baby's heart rate keeps dropping. Before you ask, I used old magic to remove your baby from your past self and placed it back in you. Mamma give her the babies soul!!!"

"Oh, very well child! I will give up the child's soul, but why did you never tell me all this before?" Luella asked.

"I will tell you why later Mamma. Right now, Nicole needs to have the soul and then to wake up," Maida said. Luella then conjured up a bright blue orb and brought it toward my belly. The orb's light grew brighter and brighter until it began to absorb into me.

Everything began to fade then as Luella's voice echoed, "I am truly sorry Princess Nicole."

My eyes began to flutter open and everything was blurry, until it all came into focus. The doctor was there, with her ultrasound machine, along with Corliss, Eldon, Dayton, Knox, and Kimberley standing around with very worried looks. I tried to sit up, but the doctor pushed me back down. Looking at the doctor I asked, "Is the baby's heartbeat alright, now?"

She looked at me surprised, replying, "Yes, your baby's heartbeat is strong. It is back to normal, but how did you know?"

"Ummm... it doesn't matter. I need to speak with Dayton. Alone, if possible," I inquired.

No one said a word for the longest time until Dayton asked, "Why do you need to speak with me?"

"It is about your wife," I said. *Wife? I do not know where that came from, but the word felt right.*

Dayton stared at me for the longest time and everyone else had confused expressions. Sighing, he finally said, "Uncle Eldon, Aunt Corliss, could we have a few moments?" No one made a move, but after a few moments everyone cleared out.

Once the door closed, I waited for Dayton and when he did not say anything, I decided to be direct, "Dayton, I need to know and I will not judge you."

He sighed, before saying, "Maida was in an arranged marriage with Athelstan. She was a sweet, beautiful girl and I hated the fact that I could not have her. We fell in love and got married, in secret. It was an old vampire tradition that bound us, right down to our very souls. I tried everything I could, but my father refused to let me marry anybody other than Enya O'Shea. To be honest, I never understood why it was I had to marry her. She cheated all the time and only wanted to be with me, because I was a Prince. Enya was nothing more than a social climber as was her father and mother….

"Maida became pregnant after a while, and I tried to work even harder to get my father to let me be with someone else. All the stress made her miscarry and that is when she cast the spell to break our bond. In casting the spell, she killed herself. I still do not know what made her do it, but unlike the rest of my family, I know it was not over Athelstan. It was my fault and I do not know why she lost hope. After her passing, a part of me died with her. I devoted my life to protecting my cousin and the girl he truly loved. I even kept postponing my marriage to Enya, much to her and her parent's dismay."

I did not know what to say and started crying. What could I say to that? He has been through so much, lost so much and does not even know why. Dayton climbed on the bed and pulled me to him, shushing me. Once my crying stopped, I croaked, "I'm so sorry. I could never imagine how that must have felt."

Once I had fully calmed down, he asked, "Nicole, how did you know I was married?"

I hiccupped, before saying, "Maida was the girl I saw when we were riding. She had to show her mother the truth because she was holding this baby's soul."

Dayton got up then and began to pace, growling, "I cannot believe that enchantress would do this. Has she not done enough? She cursed my cousin and took his true love. Plus, she has been hurting you since your arrival. It is not your fault, nor Athelstan's. This is all my fault and I cannot protect you or anyone!"

Standing up, I walked up to him. I grabbed his face, making him look at me, saying, "You are *not* responsible for whatever you are thinking. There is something that we are missing and until we know everything, you must stop blaming yourself…. What did you mean by Prince?" That part finally caught up, and I had to know.

He pulled me into a hug, saying, "My grandfather was the sixth ruler of the Shade people and my uncle is the seventh. Athelstan will be the eighth Shade King and if anything happens to either of them, I will be the next King. I would have to marry Enya before that happened and that is something I do not want. Now, may I ask you something?" I nodded my head and he asked, "Why... or how... are you pregnant?"

Laughing I said, "I'm not completely sure because I still have never had sex. But, I think that Maida is the one that made it happen. She said something about it in my last vision. She mentioned using old magic to remove the baby from my past self and placed it back in me."

"Good Goddess!" he said pulling me back at arms length.

"What? What is it?" I asked, rather scared out of my mind.

He then got down on one knee saying, "I will be sure to keep you safe, Princess Nicole."

It was sweet, but I still had one pressing question, "Dayton, I know you will protect me, but what is a Cimmerian Shade person?"

He laughed, "Cimmerians are what mortals call vampires and Shades are mythical creatures of the *night*. There is a ruler for the Shade people and a ruler for the Auroral (aw-rawr-uh l) people – the mythical creatures of the *light*. Each species of mythical creatures have some form of ruler, who report to their respective rulers. Basically, if one falls under the Shade rule, then they would report to the Shade King. However, if they fall under the Auroral rule, then they would report to the Auroral Queen."

"Wait. Why does the Shade have a King and the Auroral, a Queen?"

"The Aurorals are usually led by women, rather than men. The Auroral queen is a Faerie. Sometimes, they may be led by a king, but only if the Faeries bloodline is thinned out by mortal blood and needs to be thickened by a pure blood line. In that case, the Auroral rule falls to the Merpeople, who have a king. This gets tricky, because the Merpeople are not always ruled by a king. Every twelfth generation, the king only has daughters. In the faerie clans, males are rare and in the Merpeople, females are rare."

"Ok, I am completely confused."

"It can be confusing, but with time, you will understand all of our governmental systems."

Flopping backwards on the bed and peeking through my eyelashes at him, "Great! Just great! Do I have to understand all this?" I asked while thinking, *I was never good in my government studies in high school.*

"I am afraid so. After all, before my aunt and uncle can retire, you and Stan must be completely trained to take over." He said.

"What? Why?" I freaked. *I am not the political type.*

"You are Athelstan's wife now and he is the future King. This makes you the future Queen."

"Why me? And... when did we get married, because I would remember getting married."

"The same way Maida and I got married."

CHAPTER 16

The Impossible

I cannot believe my parents! They brought in our personal doctor, Doctor Evania Vasilis, who we did not use often, because her specialty was midwifing and pediatrics. For Doctor Vasilis to be here, and treating Nicole, made no sense whatsoever.

I had been doing a grand job of avoiding Nicole and giving her the silent treatment. However, the more I avoided her the more my body felt like it was being ripped apart. My body wanted her, as did my heart, though my mind had other ideas. I found myself asking *to want or not to want.* Right now, I was trying with all my might to keep myself from running to Nicole and holding her, until I was no longer breathing. *I cannot afford to go in that direction or I may never come back.*

Just then, as Balin came into the library, I quickly made it appear like I was preoccupied with the unknown book in my hands. I moved my eyes across the lines to make it seem as though I was actually reading. After a few minutes, he cleared his throat and without looking up from my book, I asked, "Yes, Balin. What is it?"

"Your parents wish for you to join them in the dining hall, in order to know your bride a bit better," he said warily, more afraid of what I would have to say to that, than anything else. The last few days, while she had been eating in the dining hall, I avoided her by eating in the library or my room.

Annoyed, I snapped, "I shall eat in here as I have been."

From the corner of my eye, I saw him shift uncomfortably, before sighing, "Your highness, your parents wanted me to also inform you, that if you do not come to the dining hall then you do not eat, period."

"Really? They would risk that precious mortal's life by having me starve?" I asked in annoyed disbelief.

"I am sorry your highness, but that is all I am allowed to say on the matter. It is either you eat with everyone else in the dining hall, or you do not eat at all. That is the message I am to give to you," Balin spoke rather quickly, before slowly backing out. *Bloody hell! I do not know what they are thinking, however, I want nothing to do with that annoying little wench. I guess I will be starving and when I kill that little amoeba, then it will be their fault, not mine.*

Later that night, when I went to my room, I heard Dayton and the mortal talking. Dayton asked her if she knew the sex of her baby, and if it was a boy what she would name it. It was at that moment, my anger took over and all I saw was red. Bursting into my room, I took one look at Nicole, and her belly, which looked a bit different from when I saw her last. I was consumed by pure rage. Dayton stepped in front of her to protect his baby. For once, he got something I normally would have gotten first. Seething, I wanted to kill him.

Dayton growled, as Nicole moved in front of him. Before Dayton could stop her, she pressed herself right up to me. Having her that close calmed me down, but I still growled, as I glared at my cousin. My arms wound around Nicole, pulling her closer to me, despite knowing she was having my cousin's baby. I would be damned if I was going to let him, or anyone else, make love to her again, other than me.

Still growling, I felt comforted with Nicole in my embrace, which did not make any sense. I should not want to touch her, nor bed her, and yet I did. I wanted her in a way I had not wanted anybody, since Isadora was taken from me. With a sigh, Nicole said, "Dayton, I think you should go. Stan will not hurt me, but he may hurt you."

She was right, of course. I would not hurt her; however, I was going to take from her what I wanted, and no one was going to stop me, not even her. Dayton continued to growl as he left unwillingly, while I glared during his departure. The instant he closed the door, I lifted her and laid her down on our bed. Shredding the hideous pale pink, button down shirt and a pair of dark blue, sports pants from her body. I marveled at the paleness of her flesh and frowned at the slight bulge in her abdomen. I peeled off my clothes, eager to claim what was mine.

She looked surprised by my zealousness, as I covered her lips with mine. I was surprised she did not try to stop me and she even met me with equal desire. My anger dissolved the moment I knew she was mine.

I was content with Nicole sleeping next to me. It was strange how at peace I felt with what had transpired and learning that I had been her first. I should not feel this delighted, yet I sensed I needed to just accept it.

My thoughts went back to the conversation I walked in on. *There is no way for her to be with child if I just alleviated her of her maidenhood.* Sighing, I decided it did not matter, then pulled Nicole closer to me and held her with my arm over her stomach. After a few moments, I felt something move within her.

Frowning, I looked down at her belly and moved in closer to listen. I froze as I heard the heartbeat of a baby that should not already be in her. It was not possible and yet there it was. *How or when did it happen and who is the father?* Confused, I pulled away and showered. After getting dressed, I looked at her sleeping form, smiling before I left to go find my parents and Dayton to get some answers.

While walking, I could not help but obsess over the fact that Nicole was with child. *Is it even possible for her to be carrying a baby that far along? It has a heartbeat that can be heard.* I frowned then because I knew it was not possible and I doubted it is our Goddess's child. What is more, *I cannot get over the fact Nicole belongs to me and she is my wife.* The thought made me happy, because whether she was my soulmate or not, she was mine and I was not going to let anything happen to her.

Freezing, I thought about my curse. *If what my parents said about us being tied... bound..., then when the spell kills me, would it mean that she will die as well as our baby? I cannot let this happen. She does not deserve any of this. It is not her curse.*

Picking up my pace, I soon reached my father's office and walked right in. Pausing, I saw not only my parents and Dayton, but also Enya, her parents, and my uncle. My uncle, Prince Marden, looked less than happy about something. Dayton, however, looked pleasantly pleased. Whenever his father, or Enya and her parents were involved, he was never happy. Dayton looked ecstatic and I did not understand why.

The room fell silent as I walked in. Taking my place by my parents and Dayton's side, everyone stared at me. Smirking, I said, "Do not stop on my account."

My uncle then sneered, "Well, if it is not our cursed Prince. What is it that we owe such a great honor for you to grace this conflict with your presence?"

I lifted an eyebrow because my uncle had never once liked me, unlike his son. However, that was probably because he wished he were King and not my father. Ever since my curse he simply looked down on me. I could care less, but all the same, I snapped, "Be careful, Uncle. I am still *The* Prince and your superior. I am not gracing you with anything, as I wish to speak with my parents and cousin without you lot here. However, I can wait, as I am more interested in what is going on here."

Dayton tried to hide his smile and to keep his face straight, however, I could see through the facade as it was something my father had taught me long ago. He then said, "It would seem that Enya here is pregnant, and I am not the father. The stable boy got her pregnant and seeing as we are to be married, it breaches the contract, making it null and void. However, Enya's parents believe that it does not change a thing and the marriage should continue. Enya claims she wishes to have an abortion and does not want this child."

I frowned, and asked, "Is that not why people get abortions to begin with? If she did go ahead with the abortion, it would make the contract nullified because we would never trust if the kids you two had together were yours, or not. Nor, if she will kill other unborn children that may be yours. It would make sense to me, if Dayton was freed of the contract and allowed to marry someone of his choosing. I do believe arranged marriages are a bit passé now a day, anyway." No wonder Dayton looked pleased. He has finally escaped that awful marriage contract.

Enya and her parents stood up, and glared at me, before leaving. My uncle stayed though, wanting to know what I had to discuss with his son and my parents. Folding his arms, he said, "Thank you, nephew for the help, but anything you can discuss with your parents and my son, you can discuss in front of me as well. Since, once you are gone, my son and I will be next in line." Looking to my father for help, as I did not want to discuss this with my uncle present, my father just shrugged. *What a big help? I guess, I have no choice in the matter.*

Sighing, I said, "Very well. Dayton, I want to know what you and my wife were talking about before I entered my room. I know she was a virgin, however, how is she pregnant? I do not understand. The two do not add up."

Dayton, and my parents stared at me, however, my uncle shouted, "You have married a woman carrying another man's baby? Are you insane?!

Not only have you been cursed, you risked another woman's life and that of her child's. What were you thinking and what were you two doing to allow such a thing? If it was…"

At that, my father interrupted, "Now wait one-minute Brother! It is not what you think. She is the one who married him and they both, unknowingly, invoked the old traditions. We found out she was pregnant after they performed the ritual. She is…" looking at me, he corrected himself, "was a virgin and it was Maida Miller, who put the baby in her. We are not sure why Maida used an old spell to do it, nor whose baby Maida put in her." I smiled with great pride as my father put my uncle in his place.

Dayton smiled and congratulated me, "I am glad you finally consummated your marriage."

I smiled at my cousin replying, "It was only a matter of time. What do you mean my ex-fiancé, Maida, put a baby in Nicole? I do not understand why, nor how, she could do it, seeing as she is dead."

My father, who had been beaming with pride, frowned saying, "Maida was the product of a wizard and an enchantress, not to mention the enchantress was the product of a warlock and a sorceress. Maida always had such great power, but because of her illness, she could never live to her full potential. I would imagine, in death, she is far more powerful than she had been in life. As for her reasons, I am not too sure on the answer. However, what we do know, is it had something to do with her mother and the curse placed on you."

Frowning, *I do not understand why Maida would place a baby in Nicole, or more importantly, whose baby she placed in her to begin with?* My uncle verbalized my thoughts, "How do you know Maida impregnated your son's wife and whose child would it be?"

Dayton sighed, answering, "Athelstan's wife has the gift to see the dead and Maida has appeared to her more than once. The first time was to stop Athelstan from killing her friend. The second time was to show her mother, Luella, the truth. Maida could not simply tell Luella the truth as she was still blinded by her rage and was holding the baby's soul captive. The baby would have died without it."

"Alright, fine! That still leaves the question as to who is the father? In order for Athelstan to pass the crown, the child has to be his. I do not believe for one moment the baby is his, therefore, it cannot take the crown," my uncle snarled.

My anger boiled at his comment and I grabbed him by his throat. His feet dangling in mid-air, growling, "I do not care whose baby that is inside my wife! As far as I am concerned, that baby is mine! If you or anybody else does not like it, then you can drop dead!"

Goldie walked in at that moment and placed a hand on mine saying, "You should let your uncle go. I am not sure what he has said this time, but it cannot be worth killing him."

Glaring at her for her unwanted touch, she flinched. With an animalistic growl, I said, "Get your filthy hands off me, now! Or it will not be my uncle who gets killed."

Her hand slowly let me go and my choke hold on my uncle loosened, slightly. She reasoned quietly, "Do not kill him. He is your uncle and you would regret it." When she saw I was not letting up, she added, "Would Nicole want you to kill him?" At that, I let go and stepped away.

I glared at my uncle, then turned to my parents, saying, "You deal with him because I might kill him." Storming out, I went back to my room to lay with Nicole. When I arrived, I found it empty and immediately went to search for her.

Not finding her anywhere, I panicked and went to find my parents in the dining room, as it was the last place I had yet to search. Charging into the dining room, I rushed straight to Dayton and grabbed him asking, "Have you seen Nicole?"

Frowning, he said, "I have not seen her since you got all angry and had your fun with her." He smiled at the end of his sentence.

Any other time I would have laughed, but panic filled me. I pulled him up from his seat, shouting, "I last saw her before I found you in my parent's office, all happy over your annulled marriage contract. We have to find her, *now!*"

His smirk changed to worry as he nodded, agreeing, "Yes, we *will* find her."

CHAPTER 17

The Kidnapping

I woke up, because I felt cold and tried to find warmth in Stan, however, he was not there. It caused a sharp pain in my chest that I had not felt, since I caught my ex-fiancé, Timothy, cheating on me. The pain felt much more intense now and I started crying. *I cannot believe I had given him my virginity and became another notch under his belt.* It had been wonderful, and I could fully understand why people enjoyed the act, but I felt disgusted with myself. I should not have given in. I should have fought and waited, but I cannot undo what has been done.

After I cried for a while, I decided I would get up and take a shower. However, as I stood up, I found that my lower abdomen had a soft sort of ache. It felt like I had been exercising, only that I knew I had not. Biting on my lower lip, I realized it must have something to do with the loss of my innocence. Sighing, I went into the bathroom and took a shower. Once clean, I felt a bit better... still sore, but better.

Going back in to the bedroom, I headed to the wardrobe and pulled out a pair of my black sweatpants, purple tank top that read "If Looks Could Kill I'd Be a Millionaire," and a black, Old Navy sweatshirt. Laying those on the bed, I went over to the dresser and pulled out my red bra and light blue, girl styled, boy boxers. Dropping the towel to the floor, I put on my clothes.

The moment I was dressed, a hand and rag covered my mouth. I panicked trying to get away, a natural instinct to free oneself, but I was not strong enough to break their hold and darkness consumed me.

I woke with a cotton taste in my mouth and a fuzzy, almost dizzy sensation in my head, that made me a bit nauseous. Groaning, I tried to move, only to find I was tied up. I did not know how long I struggled, however, I managed to give myself rope burns and a few deep lacerations. Quickly, I realized it was no use struggling, and gave up.

The room was dark, and I could not see much, but then again there was not much to see. There was no furniture, with the exception of the silhouette of the metal bed I was tied to. After a while of staring at the black ceiling, I heard the door open. I immediately had to shut my eyes as the light flickered on. Opening my eyes slowly, I came face to face with a girl I had never seen. She had short, curly, dark brown hair, dark brown eyes in the shape of a lemon cut in half, a long broad African nose, very plump lips, rose tinted high cheekbones, and skin the color between olive and a slightly dark golden tan.

She smiled at me, in a fake sweet way, that made me feel sick to my stomach. When she finally spoke, her voice had a nasally sound to it. In an Italian accent the woman said, "Hello Dear Princess, my name is Trilby. You made a big mistake coming to Jolly Old England to marry our Prince."

I frowned at her, "I did not come here to marry anybody."

She threw her head back cackling, very loudly, when Goldie came in with a lifted eyebrow asking, "Trilby... what are you laughing about?"

"I am laughing because Princess Nicole claims she did not come here to marry Prince Athelstan. Do you want to deal with her or should I," Trilby said?

Goldie looked from her to me, then said, "I will do it, you may go. Enya and her parents are waiting for your brother to show up. Enya is getting rather nervous having Nicole here because of how frantic both Prince Athelstan and Prince Dayton are trying to find the Princess; however, they will not find her alive."

At hearing her last statement, I swallowed tightly. Goldie and Trilby heard me gulp, as the pair smiled, before Trilby left. The voice in my head came back saying, *"Princess Nicole, be careful about what you say to Goldie. She will not just hurt you, but the baby too."*

Goldie walked closer and a chair materialized out of nowhere. Placing one leg over the other and folding her arms over her breast, she swayed her foot glaring at me. After a few moments of silence, she finally broke the void by asking, "Do you know what is going on? I hear that you are quite the little seer." I shook my head causing her to lift her eyebrow, before saying, "Since you know nothing of *our* world, I will give you the

411. The Moren family have been the rulers of our kind, for thousands of years. In the beginning, mortals and Cimmerian Shades got along. Then, mortals began to fear us, forcing immortals and magical creatures into enslavement….

"Justus Moren was newly crowned King of all Cimmerian Shades, when the last family met their untimely end. King Justus, Goddess rest his soul, had a gift that allowed him to erase the memories of others. He took a hundred guards and went from town to town, freeing all the imprisoned Shades and Aurorals, erasing the mortals memories of our kind. Once he had freed all his people and the Auroral people, the world forgot about us. We became nothing more than a myth….

"All mythical creatures are grateful to the Moren family despite some of the animosity amongst few of the creatures. We now live peacefully because of the Moren's. There was a time that we all fought, but King Justus put that to an end. He created peace, by subdividing the Shade and Auroral's peoples, who then reported back to their respective rulers. Now there are many of us mythical creatures, who wish to come out of hiding. We are tired of having to hide ourselves and know when we come out of hiding, mortals will not accept us. They will persecute and/or kill us. Our plan is to take over and enslave all of the mortal race. You, my dearest Princess have put a damper on that."

Confused, and sensing I needed now more than ever to keep her talking, I asked, "How exactly did I put a damper on that?"

She then moved her leg back onto the ground and leaned forward, "You dampened it by coming here and marrying Prince Athelstan. When Athelstan is married to his twin soul, the curse on him will be removed and free him to ascend the throne. With you married to him, that means Dayton cannot be King and as of a few hours ago, is no longer going to marry Enya. If Dayton had just married her centuries ago, then we would not have had to change our plans. Although Enya, and her siren ways, have not helped much either. But of course, Dayton had to find love in his twin soul, Maida, and marry her. I had to make sure that ended fast. The damn fool had to go and marry him, in the old traditions, just as you have…." Her cell phone interrupted her little speech. Before she answered the phone, she placed a hand over my mouth to silence me. Opening her phone, she answered with a polite "Hello," then fell silent before saying,

"Yes, sir…. Right away, sir…. I am on it, sir." *Those are a lot of sirs to answer with.* Closing her phone, she sighed, "I have to go, but Trilby will be back to end you… once and for all."

Then, I heard the voice in my head tell me, *"Stall her! I am bringing you help."*

I was not sure how and voiced my thoughts, "Stall her? How? In case you have not noticed, I am tied up and cannot, rightly, go anywhere. What good will stalling her really do? From where I lay, it is only prolonging the inevitable."

Not realizing it, Goldie spun around in the doorway to glare at me. She surprised me when she growled, "Who are you talking too?"

Startled, I jumped. I was shocked when I realized I had spoken out loud. I was scared that if I did not answer her, there was no telling what she might do. Biting on my lower lip, I sarcastically said, "I am answering the voice in my head."

"Careful Nicole, do not make her mad. We will be there soon. Try not to get killed, before we arrive," the voice said. Goldie was saying something while the voice in my head had been talking.

Ignoring Goldie, I asked, "Who is we? And how soon is soon?" *What could I rightfully lose at this point?*

Goldie paused once again, glaring at me. Asking, "What do you mean by who? I am asking you what voice in your head? Are you insane?"

Rolling my eyes, "Well, if I knew the voice's name, then I could tell you. Seeing as I do not, I cannot. No, I am not insane. My sanity has been tested once before. The therapist said, 'as long as the voice was not telling me to do bad things, it was alright.' They tried medications, but those did not work. Besides, I do not always talk to it out loud, but I seem to have forgotten how to only think my thoughts. Seeing as I am already in a room with a nut job…. Truly! You are asking me if I am insane? You are the one trying to help others take over the world and enslave mankind!"

Okay, that was probably not the smartest word choice. The voice in my head was yelling at me for my smart mouth, but it did not rightly matter, seeing as Goldie moved faster than I thought possible. At the last second, I moved, trying to get more comfortable, when the knife Goldie had in her hand, plunged into my heart. Gasping for breath, I began to fill up with fear. Goldie looked pleased with herself, while I coughed up blood. I slipped into a painful unconsciousness, as someone came bursting through the door.

* * *

We had looked all over the castle for Nicole and she was nowhere to be found. I was worried and freaked out. I could not lose her! Not when I just found her! I did not know if I could stand losing her, forever. I felt like pulling out my hair and screaming, until I no longer had a voice. As I paced in the library, a shiver went down my spine. I never had a chill before and wondered where it came from. The answer to the shudder surprised me, to say the least.

"Hello, Athelstan. It has been a while since I last spoke with you, or have been heard by anyone other than your twin soul, that is." The voice came from nowhere and sounded all too familiar. Turning around, I found Maida sitting in my favorite spot. She did not look much different from the last time I saw her. However, she had a healthier glow to her skin that I had never before seen on her.

"How??? What??? Why???" I stammered, trying to form a coherent sentence, which failed. Then, I realized *I had taken both of Nicole's innocences. With seers, if a Cimmerian takes one innocence or the other, they gain the seers abilities. Nicole's abilities extend from seeing into the future, to seeing the dead. Now, I can do the same. Sweet!*

"How can you can see me, you ask? Well Athelstan, you are connected to Nicole. When Nicole married you, unknowingly - my fault by the way - she gave you her gifts, as you have given her yours. It has taken you longer to access those abilities, as you have been just as stubborn as I remember you being, if not more. To answer why, it is because Nicole is in danger. You and Dae must go and get her back. If you do not hurry, she and your son will die," she explained. The how I already knew, but I did not know the why.

"My son? You mean that baby she is carrying is, in fact, mine? How is that possible?" I asked, confused.

"Yes. When my mother kidnapped Isadora, to curse you, I followed her. I did not know how to stop my mother, however, I soon realized that your mate was with child and did the only thing I could. I removed the infant from her body, just before my mother killed her and kept the baby alive, in limbo with me, until your twin soul returned. I knew the moment Nicole crossed onto the castle, that Isadora's soul had been reborn. Nicole is carrying the child, you and Isadora conceived, nearly three hundred years ago. He is not Nicole's genetically, as she is merely a vessel. However, I foresee children in your and Nicole's future. This first boy will not be the next King, as he will give up his crown to be with his twin soul. Your second son will be the King and his twin soul will set humans free from death and enslavement. Now, you must go and save her."

I was frozen in my spot, until joy overtook me, with the knowledge that the baby in Nicole was mine, along with the knowledge that we would have more children. "Thank you, thank you, for saving a piece of my Isadora! However, why would my first born give up his crown for his twin soul? No matter who his mate is, she would be treated as a princess, and later a queen, when they were crowned."

She stood up then and shook her head, "Now is not the time. Dae and your cousin, Knox, will be in here shortly. You must go to Enya's because that is where Nicole is. Oh... do not trust Goldie, for she is the cause of all of this."

I growled as the two people Maida told me would enter, entered. Dayton quickly stood in front of me and beside Maida. "What is it Athelstan?" he asked worriedly. Maida looked sad as she stared at him. Something told me that she knew more than she was telling me.

"Where the hell is Goldie?" I growled animalistically at him.

"Goldie is out looking for Nicole on the grounds, as I instructed. Why?"

"What is going on Athelstan?" Knox asked, placing a hand on my shoulder.

"I do not know, exactly, but Maida says not to trust Goldie. The three of us must go to Enya's because that is where Nicole is." I snapped, pulling away, pacing once more. Stopping, I spun and commanded, "Call Goldie and tell her to head back to the throne room. Tell her that the castle is under attack and you need her to guard my parents. Knox, go and tell my parents the minute Goldie enters the throne room, she is to be arrested and must await trial."

Knox took off immediately, but Dayton appeared frozen. After a few seconds, he reached into his pants pocket and pulled out his phone. After speed dialing Goldie's number, we waited as three rings sounded, before she finally picked up. "Hello," she answered.

"I need you to head back to the castle and head to the throne room, to guard the King and Queen. Nicole's disappearance started some attack and I need to go to make sure the attackers are dealt with." He said in the most urgent voice.

"Yes, sir. Right away, sir," she answered.

"Make sure you stay with the King and Queen. Where they go, you go. Whatever you do, do not let them out of your sight!" He commanded.

"I am on it, sir," she said with a muffled voice in the distance.

"Make sure you do!" He said anger building in his voice. Knox came back then and nodded. *Great, now we are going to get my Nicole back.* Dayton sent a text out to his third in command and the three of us left for Enya's. *Goddess, please let us be able to bring her back safely.* I prayed for the first time in a long time.

As we came to the castle's border, I nearly stopped because I feared the pain it would cause. However, I felt the consequences would be dire and I would lose my twin soul, once again. Pushing through the castle grounds border, I felt a twinge, but no pain. Knox and Dayton gasped and looked at me. I knew they felt the curse lift, as I became free.

Enya's house came into view and we paused outside hiding in a bush, as a tall fair-skinned man came up to the door. He looked well built, with a shaved head, and wore a fine suit. It was the sort of thing that my father and Dayton wore for important matters. It had me curious as to what was truly going on.

"She is in the cellar... in a sort of cell... but, it may be too late, already. Goldie left out the back, with more blood on her hands then I care to explain. Have Dae go and get Nicole. You must talk to Enya, and her twin soul, to change the fate of all humanity and mythical creatures alike. Just keep the Americas the Land of the Free." Maida said, as she disappeared.

Angry, I looked at Dayton saying, "Dayton, Nicole is being held in the cellar. Go and get her. Knox will stay with me and we will find out what is truly going on." Dayton nodded and took off. Knox looked at me with fear in his eyes, waiting for my move. Standing up straight, I headed to the front door, with Knox in tow.

We heard yelling and growls before I knocked. Silence followed, until the door opened to reveal Mr. O'Shea, who looked rather surprised to see me. This made me happy and I smirked as he shot a glare my way. "It would seem the Cursed Prince has been freed from his spell... what a wonderful thing. Now you may take the throne." His words sounded pleased, however, his voice was anything but. Opening my mind, I began to sift through his mind and saw what he wanted and how far he would go to get it. I knew it was forbidden for Cimmerians to read other Cimmerians minds, however, it was the only way to know who to trust. Mr. O'Shea could not be trusted.

I simply said, "I came for my wife. Once I have her, I have some matters to discuss with Enya and your stable boy."

"I do not know what you are..."

"Cut it! I know you stole her and I know you have her in your cellar. Now, I want her and I would wish to speak with your daughter and her mate. Now!" I snapped, fearing it was already too late for Nicole.

"Father, we will speak with him. You and Mummy should go get Nicole." For once, Enya spoke nicely, which scared me because of the smirk on her lips and the twinkle in her eyes.

Mr. O'Shea stepped to the side, opening the door wider, letting us in. He and his wife left, as Enya led us into their living room. A tall, dark skinned, muscular man stood behind the chair in which Enya sat. She crossed her ankles and placed her hands neatly, on her knees, waiting for me to speak.

After a few, long moments of silence, I spoke, "Very well. Since it is taking them a long time to get my Nicole, I will cut to the chase. I know what you are planning to do and as I thoroughly disapprove, I will make you an offer. One I suggest you take, because if you do not, we will lose a lot of good Shade lives, needlessly, including yours."

The man, I assumed was the stable boy, moved quickly in front of me. As he went to grab my throat, Knox quickly pulled his sword out, placing it right up to his throat. Enya let out a gasp, before whimpering, "Please do not hurt him. We will listen to your deal. If it is something that we both think is good, then we will agree to the terms."

"The deal is this: I will give you, and your new husband, the title of King and Queen of most of the Shade world."

They shared a look and simultaneously asked, "Of most of the Shade world?"

"Yes, most," I answered, "My family will move to the Americas. We will set up a place where mortals, Shades, and Aurorals can live, in harmony. You will rule the rest of the Shade world, but the Moren's will rule over those living on the free continents."

"No way!" The stable boy said, "We get it all or nothing!"

"Then, you will get nothing. You will be charged with treason and sentenced to death." I said.

Enya stood and placed a hand, on her mate. "Phomello, we must think about our baby. This is his suggestion and we can make counter suggestions, as well. That is how you make a deal and agree on all the terms." He nodded, and she continued, "Fine, but we want the castle and you out of it by morning."

"Alright, but we will get a fortnight to get all our belongings out, before you move in." I held out my hand to seal the deal. Knowing they were going to double cross us and only give us until midnight to remove ourselves and our personal items, I started to make plans in my head.

"Deal," Phomello said, taking my hand.

After we shook, sealing our agreement, Enya's parents returned with Nicole. She was crying, rather hard, and had her arms around herself, as if trying to hold herself together. It broke me and I growled, "What, happened?" *Someone is going to pay for hurting my wife and child.*

CHAPTER 18

The Sacrifice

I had always wondered what dying would feel like. It was something I never wanted to experience again. The end was rather peaceful, though, the beginning hurt far too much. I was standing in a dark, warm place, surrounded by fog, wondering what was going to happen. *Am I waiting to be judged before going to heaven, hell, or reborn into the world?* It was not long before someone appeared. *I'd rather be left alone in the dark.*

Maida's mother, Luella, appeared wearing a sad expression. Part of me wanted to run, but another part wanted to tell her to go away. I decided to stay put and see what happened.

She shook her head and folded her arms, over her chest. "Nicole, I am sorry for what has happened. It is important for you to not give up on life. Try to think of your baby and Athelstan."

Tears welled up then, "Why should I live for him? He does not care about me and I am just another notch on his rather long bed post." My tears spilled over and ran like the Nile River.

Luella wiped at my tears. "Child, he does care. You are his twin soul, after all. That is why I was trying to scare you off. Although, I may have gone a bit overboard on the task and for that, I am truly sorry."

I wanted to say *yah think* but reframed from doing so. Instead, I asked, "So, what happens now if I do not want to be dead, that is? How do I live again?" *I can live for my baby's sake, but I do not know if I can live for Stan.*

She laughed then. "Well, at the moment, we are waiting for Prince Dayton. Once he shows up, you can go back to your body."

I wanted to ask many questions, but I was unable to make any sounds. Silence followed. After a few moments, Dayton showed up and Maida popped in, a little while later. However, I ended running and jumping up into Dayton's arms for a hug.

"Nicole, now is not the time for this. You have to go back!" He said, sounding rather serious and setting me on the ground.

Nodding my head, I said, "Yeah… ok, but how do I do that exactly?"

"We will all guide you." Maida said with a sad look. I nodded my head, wondering how they were going to guide me back to my body.

"Close your eyes, child, and empty your mind. You will be back in your body, soon enough." Luella said, as the three of them encircled me, taking hands. Figuring that I should do as I was told, I closed my eyes. However, emptying my mind was harder to do than I thought, but I finally managed.

Taking my first breathe hurt more than dying. After I got my breathing back to normal, I opened my eyes. Dayton stood at my right, as Maida and her mother stood at my feet. Sitting up I was surprised that I could. The ropes, that had bound me, laid untied on the ground. Also, on the ground was a large pile of grey powder, which confused me. Looking from it to Dayton, I realized that Dayton was no longer alive. Somehow, I knew that pile of ashes was him.

Tears swelled in my eyes, but I pushed them back, asking, "How??? Why???"

"Ssshhhh…. Nicole, it had to be done. This has nothing to do with the fact that you need to…" he began, only to stop mid-way, as two people I had not met walked in.

The woman was a little shorter than myself, with almost translucent skin, green eyes, oddly plump lips, blonde hair, with a face and body of a model. She stayed by the rooms door, while the man entered. He was tall and stocky with black hair, tan skin, dark brown eyes, thick cheekbones, a broad, almost flat nose, and thin lips. He did not look attractive, in the least.

Reaching out a thin, yet beefy hand, the man said in a British accent, "Come Princess, His Highness is awaiting you."

Dayton growled, as I moved my hands away from the man and behind my back. This man felt serial killer kind of evil. After a few moments of staring at his hands, I answered shaking my head.

"Damn it girl! I have no time for this! Prince Athelstan and Knox are upstairs now waiting for you. Either come the easy way or come the hard way. Either way, you will be coming with us."

Dayton growled, once more, but I stayed where I was, shaking my head. When I finally found my voice, I said in a squeaky whisper, "I am not leaving without Dayton."

This time, the woman lost her patience and with an angry, shrill voice, snapping in a British accent, "If you happen to look around *Princess, Prince Dayton* is nowhere in here! Now, come!" She snarled the words Princess and Prince Dayton, like we were a deadly disease.

Dayton growled, "That is half true. My body is no longer here, but my ashes are and my soul, too." He looked at me and his face softened, saying, "Nicole, you should go with them. If Athelstan sent them, then he had a reason for doing it."

I shook my head, saying, "No, I am not leaving without you!"

Maida came to stand next to Dayton. Placing her hand on my shoulder, she began to plead, "Please Nicole..."

I firmly said, "No!" *I cannot leave Dayton in this awful place.*

"Princess, who are you talking to?" The man said, annoyed, figuring I was not talking to either of them.

"Dayton, Maida, and Luella," I snapped, rather angrily.

"Stupid girl! Dayton is not here, and those stupid, pathetic witches are not either." The woman said, walking into the room and grabbing my hand, roughly, pulling me from the metal bed. Nearly falling, as she pulled me towards the door, I was trying and failing to free my hand she had trapped in a vice like grip. Dayton growled, and Luella was then in front of us. She grabbed the woman's hand, ripping it away from me, before throwing her into the man, sending them both to the ground.

"Honey, are you alright?" the man asked, worried. His wife nodded her head and he turned to glare at me, snapping, "You had no right to hurt my wife like that! We just want you out of here, so that we can regroup and make new plans!"

Dayton and Maida stood next to Luella, forming a barrier between myself and the couple. Dayton looked to me and asked, "Will you tell them we do not want them touching you?" I nodded my head, but before I could say anything, he added, "Nicole, you must follow the O'Shea's up to Athelstan and Knox. Inform Athelstan about my remains. He will have them taken care of and buried properly." Tears swelled up in my eyes, but I nodded my head.

"I will go with you, but you must not touch me in any way, because Dayton, Maida and Luella will toss you like rag dolls, if you do," I squeaked the last part, as I did not want Dayton to be dead. He had become like a big brother. He was easy to talk to about things that I did not talk about anymore. Knowing his life had somehow ended, and I was the cause, gave me a heavy feeling in my heart.

The couple, suddenly, looked rather scared. They stood up silently and skirted around me, out of the room. I followed, as I wrapped my arms around myself, trying to hold it together. I could not make it, as I started to cry, moments after leaving the cell I was in. My vision got so blurry, I could not pay much attention to where they were leading me, but I could sense the three ghosts following close behind.

They stopped in an entryway and I stepped to the side of them. No sooner had I moved, I heard Stan growl, "What… happened?"

At that moment, I did not care if he liked me or not, he was far safer than these people and I ran to his arms. His arms instantly went around me as I sobbed into him. He stroked my hair until the sobs stopped, at which point I saw a sad Knox step next to Stan, holding a canning jar filled with the gray ash. I knew it was Dayton and my crying started up again. Stan picked me up into his arms and I wrapped my arms around his neck, continuing to cry into his shoulder.

* * *

When Nicole ran to me, I instinctively wrapped my arms around her, needing her close to me. She cried harder than I had ever heard a girl cry before, and that pissed me off. After a few moments of silence, I heard her say Dayton's name. My head snapped up and I glared at the O'Shea's asking, "Where is my cousin Dayton? I sent him to get Nicole, before I sent you."

They both looked at one another, before Mr. O'Shea said, "We did not see him down there, but she was talking with people that we know to be long deceased." Fear prickled at my neck and I looked to my cousin Knox.

Knox stepped forward, demanding, "Show me where you held Princess Nicole!" Mr. O'Shea turned and gestured for Knox to follow. Silence fell over the room as they left, apart from Nicole's sobbing. Knox returned a while later with a jar of grey ash. When Knox returned Nicole started to cry harder. I frowned, not understanding why my cousin held a glass filled with ashes, nor why it upset Nicole. My confusion dissolved when I saw Dayton, Maida, and Luella appear beside Knox. I knew that my cousin was no longer alive, which explained why Nicole was so upset.

I was about to growl, when Dayton said, "No Athelstan! Not now! Get Nicole home and pack up the castle to move to the Americas. The world will need a place to be free and not afraid of who or what they are. More importantly, Nicole will need to know you care about her because you have not shown her any sort of *real* affection. I will explain what happened me later, but it is time to go, now!"

I picked Nicole up into my arms to head back to the castle because it was not wise to argue with the dead. Walking back, Nicole cried the whole way until she fell asleep. When we reached the castle, I took her right up to our room, while Knox took Dayton's ashes to the throne room. Laying her down on our bed, I wanted to curl up next to her and stay there forever. However, there were things that needed to be done and being in bed, would not accomplish them.

Laying a kiss on her lips, I whispered, "I will be back before you wake this time, I promise." Reluctantly, I walked out of our room and headed to the throne room. On the way, I stopped several servants and told them to start packing the castle because we were moving to the States.

As I reached the throne room, Balin was there, looking rather nervous, pacing in front of the doors in the entryway. "Bae, I need to talk with my parents, uncle, and cousin's, but I need you to get all the servants and guards working on packing up the castle."

Balin froze, blinking at me a few times at using my old nickname for him, before saying, "Your Highness, you have no idea what has been happening since you left. When Goldie came in to guard your parents, they had her arrested for treason. She fought the guards who tried to grab her. Hallward was killed by her. He was retiring from being a guard in another couple of weeks and planned to spend a few years with his grandkid. Lady Kimberley's boyfriend, Steinar, was severely hurt. He is still in the hospital wing and Lady Kimberley is with him. I will never be making Lady Kimberley mad. She shredded Goldie into confetti. The housekeepers are still cleaning up the mess...

"Knox came in, not long ago, with a jar of ashes. He said they are what is left of Prince Dayton, however, he does not know what happened to him. Your uncle is devastated, and your parents are rattled. No one knows what is transpiring and the staff are asking me questions I cannot answer. Did you just call me Bae? You have not called me that since you were a kid?"

"Yes, yes I did call you Bae. The reason Goldie was arrested is because she was part of a plot to overthrow us. I do not know what happened to Dayton, but I should shortly. However, right now I need you to get all of the workers, who are not already busy, working on packing up the castle. My parents, Knox, Kimberley, Uncle Marden, Nicole and myself *must* leave for the States tonight. I need you to get our plane fueled and ready for us to fly out, within the next hour. As for why, it will be explained later, as I know more. For now, all I can tell you is, I gave power to most of the Shade world, to Enya and her new husband. Come morning, the only safe place for us is the States. However, we do have a fortnight to have our belongings packed and moved out."

Balin turned pale, before quivering, "Wh-why would you do that?"

"It was the only way I could save Nicole and keep us safe." I stated sadly.

CHAPTER 19

The Escape

Balin took off, doing as I instructed. Reaching for the door to the throne room, a hand fell on my shoulder. My surroundings changed, and I was in a dark room. Hearing a groan, I whirled around to the noise. Silence followed, before I heard struggling and the faint scent of blood filled my nose. *I know that scent.... I have tasted that blood.... It is Nicole.*

Anger bubbled in me at the thought of my beloved bleeding. *I am going to seriously mangle whoever is hurting her.* Then, the door opened and immediately the lights were flipped on. The room was plain and the only furniture inside was a metal bed that my love was tied too. Standing in the doorway was a girl with short, curly, dark brown hair, dark brown eyes and looked a mix of Asian and African heritage.

She smiled a fake, sweet smile that made my skin crawl. When she spoke in her Italian accent, it had this nasty nasally sound to it. The woman said, "Hello Dear Princess, my name is Trilby. You made a big mistake coming to Jolly Old England to marry our Prince."

I growled at her words. *Nicole did not know this was going to happen once she got here, nor what she was doing when she inadvertently invoked the old ways.* I was too caught up in my thoughts to hear what happened when Goldie entered the room.

Goldie, broke my thoughts, saying, "I will do it, you may go. Enya and her parents are waiting for your brother to show up. Enya is getting rather nervous having Nicole here because of how frantic both Prince Athelstan and Prince Dayton are trying to find the Princess; however, they will not find her alive." My body was shaking with anger as I could not do anything to help. I knew then, this was what happened to my other half, when she disappeared.

I heard Nicole gulp as Trilby nodded and left. Then, there was a whisper that seemed only Nicole and me could hear, *Princess Nicole, be careful about what you say to Goldie. She will not just hurt you, but the baby too.* I knew that voice... it was Maida.

Goldie sat folding her arms over her breasts, glaring. After a few moments of silence, she finally asked, "Do you know what is going on? I hear that you are quite the little seer." Nicole shook her head and Goldie lifted an eyebrow, before saying, "Since you know nothing of *our* world, I will give you the 411...." She started telling Nicole about the first Moren to rule over the Shade Kingdom, then finished the tale, "Now, there are many of us mythical creatures, who wish to come out of hiding. We are tired of having to hide ourselves and know when we come out of hiding, mortals will not accept us. They will persecute and/or kill us. Our plan is to take over and enslave all of the mortal race. You, my dearest Princess have put a damper on that."

I knew of them wanting to take over, but to enslave all of the mortals???
My Goddess!

Then I heard Maida's voice whisper, "*Stall her, I am bringing you help.*"

Nicole questioned her, "Stall her? How? In case you have not noticed, I am tied up and cannot, rightly, go anywhere. What good will stalling her really do? From where I lay it, is only prolonging the inevitable."

Goldie's shoulders stiffened before she spun around in the doorway asking angrily, "Who are you talking to?"

If you only knew.

Nicole bit her lower lip. I found the action cute, as she answered, "I am answering the voice in my head."

"*Careful Nicole, do not make her mad. We will be there soon. Try not to get killed, before we arrive,*" Maida whispered.

Yes, Nicole! Be careful! I had the feeling things were about to get sour and help did not arrive soon enough.

Due to Maida's talking, I had not heard Goldie and she seemed annoyed. "Who is we? And how soon is soon," Nicole asked, with a snap.

She should not have said that. What was she thinking?!

Goldie growled, "What do you mean who? I am asking you what voice in your head? Are you insane?"

Nicole rolled her eyes saying, "Well, if I knew the voices name, then I could tell you. Seeing as I do not, I cannot. No, I am not insane. My sanity has been tested once before. The therapist said, 'as long as the voice was not telling me to do bad things, it was alright.' They tried medications, but those did not work. Besides, I do not always talk to it out loud, but I seem to have forgotten how to only think my thoughts. Seeing as I am already in a room with a nut job…. Truly! You are asking me if I am sane? You are the one trying to help others take over the world and enslave mankind!"

"Nicole! That was not the right thing to say!" I shouted, frightened, as Goldie moved quickly towards her, pulling out a knife. My heart stopped still, as the knife was thrust into her chest. Goldie smiled, pleased with herself, as Nicole began to cough up blood. Even though I knew my beloved lay in our bed, my heart still broke watching her die. Tears fell, as I listened to her heart taking its final beats. Goldie left quickly, and I wanted nothing more than time to rewind, so that I could be the one to shred Goldie into microscopic pieces. My cousin is going to get the best present ever this year for Justus Day.

Dayton then came bursting through the door. "Nicole, No!" He shouted, running up to her and cutting the ropes binding her, pulling her to him. I saw she had major rope burns and deep cuts. "Nicole! Please, you cannot die! I swore to protect you and your baby. I failed before! I cannot fail again." I did not understand what he was talking about. *He has never failed anyone. He has protected us… done everything in his power to keep us all safe.*

Trying to get Dayton to see reason, I said, "Dayton, this is not your fault. Goldie is to blame. She has lied to us, to all of us. She has fooled us, all these years." Nicole was gone, and it was Goldie's fault.

Tears fell down Dayton's cheeks as he laid her back down. "I am going to make things right. I will never let my cousin feel the pain of losing his twin soul, a second time, like me." *Wait, what did he just say?* Kissing Nicole's forehead, he placed a hand on her head and one on her heart. *He cannot be doing what I think he is doing!* Dayton chanted,

> "A life so young, it has barely begun,
> A heart so pure, it beats no more,
> A *man* who loved with all his heart, lost in a single bound,
> A *man* who lived longer than he should,
> Now gives *his* life for the pure of heart."

He did! He gave his life up for Nicole! The room filled with a bright light and when it dulled I was back in the hallway. For a single moment, I was not sure if I should be happy or sad, but either way I cried. I felt like a small child, with no way of knowing what was real and what was fake. This is why Cimmerians fear Seer blood and end up losing their minds.

One thing I knew was I owed my happiness to my cousin and the sacrifice he made. Coming back to the present, I found my family standing around the opened doors. My uncle clung to the jar containing his only son's ashes. I had never seen my uncle look so broken in my entire life. They all looked at me with various expressions; most appeared to be questioning my sanity.

I brushed off the quizzical looks and quickly started explaining the deal I made with the O'Shea's. It took three times of explaining the agreement for my parents and uncle to understand what I had done. My uncle was thoroughly mad at me over the bargain, but there was nothing he could do about it. My parents agreed that I did the right thing. They divulged to us, for years now, Dayton had known of a group who had been plotting our demise. He had informed them of the matter and was keeping tabs on the faction. This news did not please my uncle in the least.

My uncle blamed me for his son's death, saying, "You could not keep it in your pants three hundred years ago and now my son had to pay for it?! How fair is that?!" He turned to my parents and snapped, "You treated my son like he was one of your guards and not a member of your family. This is all your fault! He should have been protected like the rest of us and not the one doing the protecting!"

I snapped, "Dayton wanted to be a guard and refused to be guarded himself. That is not on us! He would not have requested to be a guard in the first place, if you had not forced him to marry Enya. Just before my curse, your son tried hard to back out of the prearranged marriage *you* placed him in. He never wanted to marry Enya! I think, like me, he found his twin soul and also like me, he was unable to back out of the contract. If you must blame someone, why not start with yourself...?

"When I am King, the first thing I am doing is making an amendment in the marriage contract so that when a Shade finds their twin soul, then an arranged marriage is null and void." I was spending too much time away from Nicole and my temper was rising.

I continued to tell them what Goldie did to my soul mate and what Dayton did to save her. His sacrifice is what spared me from losing my other half, a second time. Uncle Marden was surprised to find out that his only son gave up his life for Nicole and that Dayton had found his twin soul.

I jumped when Kimberley spoke behind me, not knowing she was there as I thought she would still be in the infirmary, looking after Steinar, "Glad I sliced and diced that *bitch*. Sorry, you could not exact your revenge." I waved it off as nothing, because I was sure that if the cleaners were still cleaning parts of Goldie out of the throne room, then she made Goldie's last moments painful.

Knox growled, "I wish I could have helped in taking down Goldie." His sister looked at him and they started one of their notorious, silent conversations.

Feeling anxious and needing to be reassured my mate was breathing, I excused myself. I told my family I was going back to my room, to make sure everything I needed was packed and ready, before we had to leave. They all nodded in agreeance and left to their rooms, to do the same.

When I got back to my room, I found Nicole still sleeping. Walking in, I saw the chambermaid packing our clothes into two suitcases. She looked up as I entered, pausing long enough to bow before going back to work. Striding up to Nicole, I moved her hair from her face and noticed that she had tears stains running down her cheeks from crying. I felt so angry at that moment because I should have taken better care of her.

Climbing into bed, I pulled Nicole into me because I wanted to make sure she was truly still alive. Having her gifts was a real eye opener and I needed to make sure *she* was real. *I will need to control this gift, even if it is the last thing I do. For now, I will enjoy what I have; a beautiful wife and a son on the way. A son, who will one day live a life without fear of any kind. A son who will know love and know what it feels like to hold his twin soul.*

Feeling the need for conformation of reality, I listened into both Nicole and our baby's heartbeats. However, I became confused when I heard an extra heart thumping. Looking up I saw Maida and Dayton. Maida appeared to be guilty and Dayton seemed sad.

Right when I was about to speak, Dayton interrupted saying, "Just listen, Stan. *Do not* say a word."

When I nodded my response, he looked to Maida. "Athelstan, I did not only place *your* child inside Nicole. I also placed mine and Dae's son in her as well."

A growl rumbled through my chest, as she took a step back. *How dare she use my mate?!* Dayton spoke before I could snap back, "Let her finish, Athelstan."

"I am sorry... it was selfish using your mate like this, however, when I died I did not know I was pregnant again. I had hoped to place our child inside Enya, once Dae married her. When Nicole showed up as the reincarnation of Isadora, I knew I was going to place your child in Nicole and I saw it as a chance for our child to be born, as well. Please do not be cross with me." Maida seemed to be cowering behind Dayton the more she spoke.

Whispering quietly, "I am not mad... I am pissed!!! However, seeing as Dayton and you have saved my twin soul.... You are forgiven."

Nicole moved closer to me and it released my anger. Maida and Dayton smiled before fading as Balin and the chamber maid came over to our bed. As they stared at us in silence, I somehow knew there was a problem and wished I had more time to spend with my beloved in our home. Then again, my home had been a prison for me for hundreds of years. *I am now free. Free to see how much the world has changed, in person. I guess I shall start seeing the world in the Americas.* The chambermaid bowed to me and left.

Balin stood there silent for a while longer before saying, "Your Highness, you and your parent's belongings are packed, as well as most of the castle. I have made arrangements for a mover to come in the morning and load everything. The jet is fueled and ready to fly you to the States. The car is ready for you and your family. Is there anything else you would like me to do?"

I was about to say *no* when I remembered what I had learned about the faction, saying, "Yes! You need to tell all the staff that there is a change coming and our hidden world is about to come out in the open. When it does, no mortal will be safe. Tell them if they wish to live in harmony with mortals, then they will need to pack up their belongings, and move to the States. Balin, tell them to share this information with their families, as well. I will see to it that all their belongings are moved to the Americas.... Also, tell them I will help them find new homes and new jobs."

"Sir, is this part of the deal you made with Enya and her husband?" he asked, with worry and fear on his face. I knew the fear came from the fact that his youngest son had found his twin soul, a mortal, and had yet to tell her about his people. Now her race was about to be captured and enslaved.

"No. That is not part of the deal, and before you ask, I know this because I have gained a few extra talents. These skills come from Nicole. Thanks to her abilities, I now know what happened to Dayton. He gave his life for Nicole because Goldie killed her before she was found. Before that, Goldie told Nicole of our past and of the plans her faction has plotted for the future of the whole world. Basically, their plans are for all mythical creatures to come out of hiding and enslave all mortals, as we were enslaved long ago," I told him.

He nodded, asking, "What about the rest of the mortals on this planet who do not have the luxury of this knowledge?"

"Right now, we will get ourselves settled in the Americas. When our mythical world comes out, we will need to sit with the government officials to sort out a new way of life for all creatures involved. This may result in us swiftly sorting through the mortal's minds to determine who we can and cannot trust. There may be a lot of push back and it will need to be resolved quicker than the mortal constables are capable of handling."

I got out of bed, and wrapped my blanket around Nicole, before lifting her up into my arms and carrying her out to the waiting car. Balin followed, as he would be seeing us off before coming back and fulfilling my requests. Before reaching the entrance, he said, "I suppose that is for the best. It is a little overwhelming, your Highness, not being able to tell the mortal world what is coming." I knew how he felt, but there was nothing we could do to help them at this time. Right now, my thoughts were simple: *what will be, will be and what will happen, will happen in the end.*

Walking down the stairs and through the front door, I descended the front steps. As I reached the bottom, the O'Shea's came storming up. Mr. O'Shea shouted, "Hold it right there! You may not leave here with anything as it now belongs to us!"

Looking from him, to Enya and her husband, I lifted an eyebrow saying, "We agreed that my family and I have a fortnight to have our belongings packed and moved. You have no right to make such demands, now!" The last part I shouted angrily.

Enya smiled evilly, before saying, "Yes, however, seeing as the castle is now ours, we do not want you to remove any of our new belongings. Besides, you never got it in writing. Therefore, it is ours."

Smiling, I shouted, "Guards!" It took less than half a second, for thirty guards, to surround them. I passed Nicole to Balin, with resistance on my part. He took her, carefully, as not to wake her and handed her to my father, sitting in the car. Storming over to where the O'Shea's stood, I smirked growling, "You may think that all you like, however, the moment you took my hand, our contract was sealed. My unique power allowed me to create a written contract the moment the deal was struck. A copy of our agreed upon terms is sitting, signed by both parties, in the throne room." My smile grew as I pulled out the original copy and continued, "I have here the original document."

Mr O'Shea tried to grab the parchment, however, a guard drew her sword and flashed it under his nose. "You honestly think you can get your hands on the original copy that easily?" I paused, looking him up and down. Frowning, "You wanker! Well, I guess you gave me no choice. You will be placed under house arrest, until all of the Moren family heirlooms and furniture have been safely removed. Thane, escort these tossers home until a fortnight has past."

Thane Ward nodded his head to each of the royal guards, who took each O'Shea member hostage and led them back to their home. Thane turned towards me, placed a fist over his heart and bowed, slightly, saying, "Your Highness, we will keep them under house arrest, but with all due respect, are we to be governed by them?"

Shaking my head, I answered, "It is your choice if you wish to be employed by them, but you may continue to work for my family. I cannot explain more, at this time. However, Balin will inform all the workers about what will be transpiring. I will tell you that if you care to remain head guard of the *true* royal family, I would get ahold of your wife and tell her to start packing up your belongings to move to the Americas. Once you know what is happening, if you have any close family or friends, who you believe to be absolutely loyal to us, share this information with them and advise them to move as well. I leave everything in both Balin and your capable hands." I got in the car and my father gave me Nicole. The moment the door closed, the driver sped off at Cimmerian speed.

When we arrived at the airport, we unloaded the car and boarded the jet. Nicole remained asleep and I did not let her go the entire flight. I did not even set her down when Clarence came and told me I needed to put her in her own seat. I flashed a Cimmerian glare at him and held her tighter. I could not let her go. I needed her in my arms. I needed validation to know that she was still here. Still alive and this was all really happening.

After the pilot announced that we were free to roam the plane, my father and uncle came closer to where I sat. We did not need to state the obvious as to what was needed to be talked about. There were a great many details to go over about the faction and to figure out what we could do to live peacefully with mortals.

It was decided that the Americas should remain the land of the free and we would need to bring other Shade tribes, clans, and packs who live in harmony with the mortals. We understood our family maybe hit hard financially, but it would be worth it in the end to keep as many mortals out of enslavement as we could.

By the end of our discussion, my father and uncle both agreed, "You made the right decision and we cannot be prouder of you. If this faction had killed off our family line, there would be no safe place for *any* mortals to live."

As my father said this, my uncle nodded, before adding, "You are finally starting to think like a ruler and not thinking with your prick." It was almost a compliment from my uncle, so I was willing to let it go, for now. However, I knew he would, at any moment, make a comment to make my blood boil. I smirked, thinking about the extra surprise in my beloved and decided to save that little piece of information for when he did piss me off.

The flight took about eight hours to get from the United Kingdom to the east side of the United States. After we refueled, it took another five hours to get to the valley where Nicole lived.

She finally woke up when we first landed in the States, however, she did not speak. She would not, or could not, look at anyone even if they called to her. When she finally took her own seat, I pulled her to me and held her once more. I was beginning to worry about her because she felt hollow, like an empty shell.

* * *

When I woke up, I was not in the castle anymore. Instead, I was on a plane, and confusingly in Stan's arms. We sat on the same couch I had woken up on before and I did not know how I had gotten here, nor why. My body felt numb, almost hollow and my voice was dry, constricted. I knew of the people around me, but not who they were. At times, I heard them call out my name, but I could not answer. *How could I, when I should be dead… not Dayton?*

After a while, I moved to my own seat next to Stan. He immediately pulled me closer to him and wrapped his arms protectively around me. It was that action that made me feel safe and loved, but did he love me or was he using me to ascend to the throne?

I knew not of where we were headed, and I was not sure if I cared. Sometime later, we landed, and peoples voices started to register in my head. Stan lifted me into his arms and walked us off the jet. I heard a slightly familiar voice ask a question, but I did not understand. I did hear Stan say, "It is going to cost us quite a bit, but we need to have a place that can allow us to live with them…. I can get a job to cover any other costs." Then, I heard someone else say they would get one too. A chorus then rung out with the same responses.

"Why would you need to get a job… or more money? Stan, if we are truly married, as I have been told, then what is mine, is yours. I make a bit from the houses, apartments, and rooms I rent out each month and I own a piece of land. I have been slowly building my dream home, to open a Bed and Breakfast." My eyes moved to Stan's face and he had a look of relief. I did not know why he looked relieved, nor the cause.

Then, he kissed me passionately. Stars exploded, and fireworks went off. I had never had a kiss like this in my life. I knew then, I had my happily ever after. Though, it did not last long…

EPILOGUE

The True Happily Ever After

After Stan's family and I were State-side, we finished building my Bed and Breakfast. It ended up bigger than I anticipated and quickly turned into a hotel. This hotel became the new Moren family homestead. It took some time and doing, but we got all the Cimmerian Shades and their human spouses to the Americas.

Then, all hell broke loose, as our mythical existence came out and thousands of lives were lost. The humans who embraced our existence, lived free of fear. However, those who feared and hated us, were captured and expelled to foreign lands to be subjugated. There was pandemonium, for over a hundred years, in the outside worlds.

The O'Shea's rule was short lived, as they were killed and overthrown by the Sheridon clan. The eldest son took over as King and the family was far more ruthless, than the O'Shea's. Not many humans made it to the Americas after that. Those who did, were lucky. Now, the subjugated humans were nothing more than blood banks. They were treated as bad, if not worse, than the Africans during their enslavement.

In the chaos, more mythical creatures lost their ability to procreate, with no reason why. There had been studies conducted to find a solution to this problem.

However, until then enslaved humans were being forced to breed for them. Their babies were taken and converted to carry both their creator's genetics. The children were usually infants, but no older than three, because it had been discovered children over three could remember everything from before their transformation. This caused rebellion because they remembered the horror, the death, the fear, and the pain.

As time passed, Athelstan and I had to teach ourselves to master our talents, as there was no one with our abilities to guide us. It took us many years to gain the knowledge needed to help the mortals, whose lives ended abruptly. They were the hardest to help, because they carried the most afflictions and hatred. We discovered the best way to help these spirits move on, was to ask the Cimmerian Goddess to guide the lost souls to peace.

Our son was born first. We named him Dayton Harvard Moren II because he would not be alive if not for Dayton Harvard Moren I. His twin, and cousin was named, Theodore Merlin Moren. The four of us fought over names because Stan and I felt I had a right in naming him as I was the one to carry him. Maida and Dayton conceded to Theodore, after I gave them a list of names I was thinking about. However, Maida insisted that his middle name had to be Merlin, as it was her great, great grandfathers name.

For years, we both saw Dayton and Maida as they helped us make a free world. After the birth of our second child, Lamont, we never saw them again.

Our last child, whom we named Rapunzel, as I passed the age of conception. She was a beautiful little girl, with dark red curls and pale skin, and deepest sea blue eyes I had ever seen. Athelstan always teased that she was of the Merpeople. I did not find it funny, as the Merpeople King hated those who walked on land and breathed air.

She frightened us, though, as she often slipped in and out of a comatose state. The doctors feared she would never see her sixteenth birthday. We hoped that she would but were preparing for the worst. Papa Eldon has said he knew of a witch who could help us but feared that an older family curse was what ailed her. If that was the case, then there would be a way to break the curse.

Dayton II abdicated his right to be King of the Americas, as Maida told Athelstan he would. However, the reason as to why was outstanding and made me so proud.

His brother, Lamont, came to accept the ascension, but only after he met his true mate. Both Athelstan and I began to wonder if he was ever going to settle down.

Although, Athelstan always said he would settle down, when he met the right girl like he had... *twice.* That concept had taken me a long time to accept as Athelstan teased me about having me, not once, but twice, as a virgin in two different forms. It confused me as I had not believed in reincarnation. Whenever I started to think about it, I would end up with a big headache. I tried to accept everything for what it was and to not think about my past life, too much, by focusing on the life I was currently living.

In time, our children had children, but we never met them, as our bodies had reached their non-aging limits. We retired to a better place; a place where we finally got to live our most, never ending, *happily ever after*.

The End

ABOUT THE AUTHOR

Edie Hober (ee-dee hoe-berr) grew up in a small town in Oregon. She is the oldest of three and spent most of her childhood playing on her grandparent's farm. Edie graduated from Lane Community College with two degrees in English Literature. She has a cat, Morelli, who is a Scottish Fold and a complete nutball. Edie likes to crochet and sew when she isn't writing. She enjoys taking trips to the coast and finds peace in the outdoors, camping and swimming.

Printed in the United States
By Bookmasters